WILLOW RUN

Dorothy Stephens

Dorothy Stephens

WILLOW RUN
Copyright © 2019 by Dorothy Stephens

ISBN: 978-1-68046-840-3

Melange Books, LLC
White Bear Lake, MN 55110
www.melange-books.com

Published in the United States of America.

Cover Design by Caroline Andrus

CHAPTER ONE

Willow Run Village
Fall 1951

KATE STARED OUT THE WINDOW OVER THE KITCHEN SINK, ABSENTLY rinsing suds off the dishes and stacking them on the wooden drain board beside her. Piles of dirty slush from an early snow clogged the gutters along the street outside and clung to the tops of the wooden coal boxes that loomed in front of each unit. Low-roofed, one-story buildings, each housing a half-dozen small apartments, lined the street in both directions. If she turned and looked across the cramped kitchen and through the living room window, she could see a field of scrubby weeds separating her from rows of identical buildings on the next street. Down at the corner was the bus stop, where her husband, Mark, had caught the early bus to the university that morning.

The thought of Mark conjured up an image Kate tried to shake away, but it hung there, filling her with a wave of anxiety. Amanda. Tall, blond, perfect Amanda, probably right now sitting there in class with Mark. Kate had met her at a graduate student reception at the beginning of the fall semester. Elegant in a stylish black cocktail dress, blond hair swept up in a sleek hairdo, diamond studs flashing in her ears, and an air of supreme confidence. The only woman in the Business Administration program. The hand she extended had revealed perfectly polished nails and no wedding ring. Kate tried to hide her own chipped nails and the dishpan hands that she hadn't had time or energy—or money—to do anything about.

"So are you a graduate student here?" Amanda had greeted her. "What's your field?"

Kate explained that she wasn't enrolled at the university but was there with her husband. Amanda smiled coolly, her eyes sliding away to survey the rest of the crowd. At that moment Mark appeared, carrying two glasses of punch.

"This is my husband, Mark," said Kate.

"*Mark*! I had no idea you were married. You've been keeping it a secret, how naughty." She smiled again, but this time it was directed solely at Mark, and Kate felt ignored, invisible, and subtly threatened.

"No secret," Mark responded. "Just didn't come up." He abruptly set his and Kate's empty punch glasses on a nearby table and took Kate's arm. "See you tomorrow, Amanda."

A few weeks after their first meeting, Kate had seen Amanda again at a graduate student buffet. She and Mark were helping themselves from an assortment of sandwiches, chips, and platters of limp tomatoes and lettuce when she noticed Amanda ahead of her, frowning as she poked a fork into a jar of pickles. At the same moment, Amanda glanced up and caught Kate's eye. And again, she was politely condescending.

"Oh... How are you? Kate, is it?" Without waiting for an answer she turned her intense smile on Mark. They bantered back and forth, sharing insider business school jokes, while Kate stood awkwardly by, shut out from the conversation.

Now, remembering, Kate shivered. She didn't like what she'd seen of Amanda, and she didn't trust her. Mark had seemed different lately, too. Withdrawn, maybe. Or distant? Not the old open-hearted Mark with whom she could talk about anything and everything. Now, when she mentioned Amanda he'd look away and change the subject. She tried to think positively, find excuses. Maybe he was just tired, going to school all day and working every night at the auto plant. Maybe he thought she was nagging. Or maybe he was feeling guilty. She sighed and reached for a towel to dry her hands.

A cold wind swept across the fields, worming its way through the cracks and thin siding of the apartment. Chilly drafts of air swirled across the bare plywood floor and around Kate's ankles. Pulling her sweater more closely around her, she went to check on her daughter, trying not to see the ugly government-issue chairs and couch in the sparsely furnished living room.

In a bassinet next to the monstrous coal stove that occupied one corner of the living room, four-week-old Nora whimpered in her sleep. Kate rotated the bassinet toward the stove to warm the baby's tiny toes under the layer of blankets, then stepped into the adjacent bedroom to look in on her son Robin. He'd been running a high temperature all night, and Kate had been checking on him every fifteen minutes while Mark, oblivious, had breathed heavily on the other side of their bed.

As she bent over the crib, a scream rose in her throat. Robin lay there, seemingly lifeless, his eyes rolled back in his head and his skin turning blue. She was sure he was dead. "No!" she cried out. "No, no, no!"

As she picked him up, she felt his small body beginning to stiffen, and she ran toward the front door with the vague idea of somehow finding help. For once, alone there without Mark, she was thankful that the walls were so thin. Earl, a big tough-talking construction worker from next door, had heard her screams. He burst into the kitchen and took one look at Robin. "Fill the sink with cold water," he barked. "Quick, God damn it! He's having a convulsion. We gotta bring the fever down."

Kate hurried to do as he said, her heart pounding. Earl plunged the little boy into the sink, and slowly the color began to return to his face. His eyes opened and he drew in a shuddering breath.

"Oh, thank God," Kate breathed. The wave of relief almost overwhelmed her.

"You ain't never seen a convulsion before? Our girl Lily used to have 'em when she was young."

He lifted Robin from the water and wrapped him in the towel Kate handed him. She shook her head but wasn't really listening. She was just grateful that Earl had been home and that he'd come through the door, like an angel in work boots and flannel shirt, and saved her son. Even though at first sight of him she'd had a moment of uncertainty. She'd often heard Earl shouting next door, sometimes accompanied by his angry pounding on the wall. Once there had been the sound of breaking glass as a window-pane shattered, and Kate could see the shards falling into the yard next door.

Still, Earl was here, and he was the only help she had.

She snapped back to attention when he said, "You gotta call the ambulance and get the kid to the hospital. He could go into another convulsion any minute. He's still way too hot."

In a daze, Kate ran to the telephone. Ambulance? How do you call an ambulance? She leafed frantically through the phone book for the emergency number. When she put the phone down, Earl was sitting on a kitchen chair, still holding Robin and watching for signs of another convulsion.

"Thank God you knew what to do. How can I ever thank you?" Kate's knees wobbled, and she dropped into the nearest chair, then reached for Robin. He leaned against her, his face pale and eyes drooping.

"It's nothin' I ain't done with Lily," he said. "Glad I was around. I don't have much to do these days. Got laid off." He shrugged. "Just gettin' my truck paid for, too."

He passed a hand over his hair. "Your husband is lucky to have a job on the assembly line."

It was the longest conversation Kate had ever had with Earl. Distracted by worry, she'd been only half-listening.

"I'm sorry," she said now. "I didn't know you'd lost your job."

"Nothin' anybody can do about it," he said. His shoulders slumped and he looked down at the floor.

He must be really worried, Kate thought. No wonder he sometimes loses it and starts to bang on walls.

Earl and his wife Jerilyn were from Tennessee, part of the workforce that had been brought to Michigan early in the war from all over the South to manufacture B-24 bombers at the nearby Willow Run plant. Most, including Earl, had stayed on when the plant was converted after the war to making Kaiser Fraser automobiles. Usually Kate's exchanges with both Jerilyn and Earl were limited to a 'hello' or 'how are you'?

But occasionally Robin and the couple's son Danny played together outside, running their toy cars up and down the sidewalk. Kate and Jerilyn would sit on their shared front steps while the children played and try to figure out how to talk to each other.

Jerilyn, with her frizzy red hair and freckles, her wary brown eyes, and a kind of scared rabbit look that sometimes crossed her face. And Kate, small and dark-haired, trying to be friendly. Mark always said Kate's pointed face made her look like a cute little pixie, but that's because it wasn't *his* face. And besides, who ever said being small was a good thing? She got tired of reaching on tiptoe for boxes of cereal at the grocery store, or for sweaters on the closet shelf.

But it wasn't just appearances that separated Jerilyn and Kate. Two lives couldn't have been more different. It was like conversing with someone from another planet. Kate had grown up in a peaceful suburb in Connecticut, had enrolled at the University of Michigan, where she had met Mark. Jerilyn was what some of the university students in the housing project disparagingly referred to as a hillbilly. She had never been out of her rural home in the Tennessee mountains until Earl had brought the family to Michigan early in the war.

Now, as Earl and Kate waited for the ambulance, strains of recorded music came blasting through the wall from the next apartment.

"God damn," exploded Earl. "Lily's got that confounded song playing again. I'm sick to death of it. Oughtta throw the damn record in the garbage." He got up and pounded on the wall.

"Lily," he shouted. "Shut that thing off! How many times I got to tell you?"

Though she'd cringed a little when he banged on the wall, Kate nevertheless agreed. Thanks to 12-year-old Lily, "*Side By Side*" accompanied their meals and most of their waking hours, drowning out the Beethoven and Brahms that she and Mark enjoyed.

The lines of the song ran through her head constantly, against her best efforts to dislodge them. And as if that wasn't bad enough, their bedroom shared the wall of the next door bedroom on the other side of their apartment, and she had learned more about the love life of their other neighbors, Annie and John, than she had ever wanted to know. And probably vice versa.

When a siren sounded in the distance, Kate, her knees still shaking, stood up. "I don't know what I would have done if you hadn't been here," she said.

Earl looked embarrassed. He glanced over at the bassinet. "What you gonna do with the baby?"

"I guess I'll have to take her along, if they'll let me ride with Robin. They'd better. I'm not sending him off alone. He'd be terrified."

"Tell you what. Jerry can come over here and stay with the baby, and I'll follow the ambulance to the hospital and drive y'all home."

"I can't let you do that! Or Jerry either. I'll just call a cab when Robin is released."

But Earl was already yelling, "Jerry! C'mon over here."

Jerry hurried in just as the ambulance pulled up. She hadn't had time to take off her apron, and she had thrown one of Earl's heavy jackets over her shoulders. Kate hurriedly explained about diapers and the supplementary bottles in the ice box, then with an anxious backward glance, she followed the EMTs as they carried Robin out on a stretcher. His eyes were dazed, his little body limp.

"It's all right, baby," Kate crooned. "Mommy's right here. We're going for a little ride together." His eyes focused on her face, and he tried to smile.

CHAPTER TWO

THE RIDE TO THE HOSPITAL TOOK LESS THAN TEN MINUTES. KATE STOOD IN a corner of the Emergency Room cubicle, watching as the doctor examined Robin, breathing in the hospital odors of alcohol and antiseptics and the crisp scent of clean sheets. A machine hummed from the wall, a red light blinking monotonously like a sinister evil eye.

Robin suddenly stopped breathing again and began to stiffen. Fear clutched Kate's belly, but the ER doctor clapped an oxygen mask over Robin's nose while the nurse sponged him down, and slowly the child relaxed and opened his eyes. For the second time, Kate went limp with relief.

Dr. Bevins explained that they'd like to keep Robin for a couple of hours for observation, but his temperature was already coming down and he'd probably be able to go home later in the day. Robin, exhausted, was soon asleep.

Kate sat beside his bed, leafing through a magazine while keeping an anxious eye on Robin and worrying about whether she'd have enough for cab fare to get them home. They were living on the monthly stipend they received under the GI Bill, plus what Mark earned at the Willow Run plant. There was little room for extras. Each week, she pulled the two children across the fields, in a wagon or on a sled, to the grocery store in the

Community Center. As she tossed things into the basket, she carefully added up the prices so she wouldn't go over the food budget of $20 a week.

Thinking about her scare over Robin, Kate felt mildly resentful. Why wasn't Mark ever there when she needed him? He was always either at school or working. She hardly saw him at all. No husband, no money, no car. No life. When had she agreed to this?

Immediately, guilt washed over her. Mark was working as hard as he could, studying for his MBA during the days, and putting in an 8-hour shift at night. If she was exhausted, taking care of a toddler and a newborn, shoveling coal to keep them warm, trying to figure out how to cook on a wood stove, what about him? Hitching a ride to work almost as soon as the bus brought him back from the university, with barely time to swallow his dinner. And besides all that, getting only a few hours of sleep at night.

When he'd first started working at the plant, he'd described to Kate how mind-numbing it was. "It's got to be one of the most boring jobs in the world," he said. "I stand there, hour after hour, plugging metal disks into the fenders of cars passing along the line. That's it, my whole job."

He said he had figured out that if he ran along the line as far as he could, plugging in the disks as he went, he could grab his book and study for a few minutes before the next line of cars came through.

A small smile crossed his face. "The other guys on the line are already calling me 'The Professor.'"

With such a schedule, of course Mark was never there.

Kate looked up when someone tapped lightly on the door. It was Earl. "So how's the kid?"

Kate blinked in surprise. "What are you doing here? I told you, you didn't have to do this."

"Aw, I had some errands in town anyway, so I figured I'd stop by and see if y'all are ready to go home."

"No," Kate said slowly. "The doctor said he wanted to keep Robin for a few hours for observation. Is Jerry doing ok with the baby? I'm so sorry she's had to stay with her this long."

"Baby's fine, been sleepin' most of the time except when she took a bottle. Jerry said not to worry. She's glad to do it. Where we come from," he added, "neighbors look out for neighbors."

"I think I would like your Tennessee, if all the people there are like you and Jerry," Kate told him.

"Don't know about that. It's just the way things are there." He pulled a slip of paper out of his pocket. "Here's our phone number. There's a pay phone out there in the lobby. Call me when y'all are ready and I'll come by to pick all y'all up. Jerry's got the baby over to our place till you get back."

He didn't wait for Kate's protests, and was out the door before she could speak.

Dr. Bevins came in a little later and said Robin's temperature had risen again. He didn't seem to have any other symptoms. As far as the doctor could tell, it was just one of those unexplained fevers, maybe a virus, but he'd like to keep Robin overnight just in case of more convulsions. Kate, her worries reawakened, used the pay phone to call Earl and ask him to let Mark know what had happened when he got home.

"Tell him I'm staying here with Robin. He'll have to stay home from work so he can take care of the baby."

"I got a better idea," Earl said. "Your husband can go on in to work. No sense losin' a night's pay. We'll keep the baby till he gets home from the plant, and I'll pick y'all up in the morning."

"Earl, that's too much to ask. Please don't feel obligated to do this."

"Forget about 'obligated.' Don't worry, Lily's havin' a ball with the baby. See you in the morning." He hung up.

Kate dozed restlessly on the cot the nurses put up in Robin's room. At about midnight, unable to sleep, she got up, went out to the waiting room, and used the pay phone to call Mark.

"Is everything okay?" His voice was anxious. "How's Robin? How are you? Earl talked me out of hitchhiking to the hospital..."

"Robin's sleeping," Kate interrupted. "He's fine. And I'm all right too. I just needed to hear your voice." She felt pent up tears threatening.

"I'm so sorry I'm not there with you, Katie."

"I know, but you couldn't help it." Kate could hear the gurgling sound of Nora sucking on a bottle. "Sounds like you're feeding Nora."

"Greedy little monkey, isn't she?" There was a smile in his voice. "I'm

9

about to put her to bed and hit the hay myself. Think you'll be able to get some sleep?"

"I'll try. Good night, my love."

After she hung up, Kate crawled back on the cot and eventually got to sleep.

The next morning Dr. Bevins said they could go home.

"Temperature's been normal all night," he said, peering over his glasses at Robin's chart. "He'll be fine now. Kids his age bounce back in a hurry. Just keep an eye on him if he spikes a temp again."

As promised, Earl was sitting in the waiting room reading Sports Magazine and sipping from a paper cup of coffee. He led them out to his truck and Kate, carrying Robin, climbed in.

"I talked your husband into goin' to work last night," Earl said. "He wanted to hitchhike to the hospital to make sure you were okay, but I told him you'd be sleeping in the room with the kid and you'd both be fine." He turned off the highway onto the road into Willow Run Village. Even after more than two years, Kate still had to look closely to find their street and unit in the maze of look-alike streets and buildings that had been plunked down during the war on the vacant fields outside of small-town Ypsilanti.

Earl steered easily into Raleigh Court and parked in front of their units. He helped Kate down from the truck and brushed off her repeated thanks. "Like I said, I got nothin' else to do till I get back on the job." He held the door open for her to enter.

"Jerry'll be right over with the baby," he said as he left. "Call us if you need anything later. I got to go see about a temporary job this afternoon, but one or other of us'll be around all day."

Kate had gotten Robin settled with some toys on the little area rug that covered part of the icy living room floor when Jerry knocked on the door. She was wearing a worn gray sweater against the November chill, and had baby Nora wrapped in a faded blanket. Kate noticed how frail Jerry seemed, so thin and pale, with circles under her eyes. She wondered if anything was wrong, but she didn't feel she could ask. They didn't know each other that well.

Jerry handed the baby over and Kate snuggled her close.

"You and Earl saved my life, Jerry."

Jerry gave a tentative smile. "It's okay. Earl's a little stir crazy from sittin' around all the time. Did him good to have somethin' to do. I didn't mind havin' him gone for a while neither." She shrugged. "He can get kinda cranky sometimes when we get on his nerves, and he starts yelling. You've prob'ly heard him." She looked down as though worried that she had said too much.

Her face had the scared rabbit look, and Kate wondered if it had anything to do with Earl. True, she'd often heard Earl shouting and punching the walls, but no screams, nothing to suggest other kinds of violence. Remembering the way Earl had helped her, she pushed away the thought.

Instead, smiling, she said, "Hey, with these thin walls, I'm sure you hear the baby crying and Robin having temper tantrums plenty of times." She laughed. "The Terrible Twos."

Jerry looked blank, so Kate tried to explain. "Some people call them that because two-year-olds are famous for saying no to everything. Wasn't Danny like that when he was two? I know Robin is."

Jerry looked away. "Yeah, I guess so. Terrible Twos, huh? I ain't never heard that before."

She started for the door, steadying herself against the wall, then turned back. "The baby's prob'ly hungry. I gave her a bottle a couple hours ago, but she only took about three ounces." She took a deep breath and let herself out the door.

Kate heard the other door close and Jerry say something to Lily, but she couldn't catch the words. What was wrong with Jerry? Was she sick?

Nora began to whimper, so Kate settled herself in her grandmother's rocking chair near the stove, unbuttoned her blouse and let the baby nurse. Her thoughts turned back to Jerry and Earl. She owed them a lot, and she wished she could think of a way to thank them. A way she could be a good neighbor like the people in Tennessee.

Nora squirmed in her arms and frowned up at Kate, her face turning red in protest. Kate switched her to the other breast, lamenting once again the fact that she didn't ever have enough milk; she hadn't with Robin either. Still, she persisted, even though she had to supplement

11

each feeding with a bottle of formula. She had wanted so much to breast feed her babies, but she hadn't gotten much help or support from her doctor. He'd brushed her off with the comment that women with her body build never produced much milk, making her feel like a flat-chested cow.

She'd gotten the same response when she tried to discuss natural child-birth. Her mother had sent her a clipping before Robin was born, about Dr. Grantly Dick-Read in England. In his book, *Childbirth Without Fear*, he wrote about something called natural childbirth, in which he advocated techniques like massage, relaxation therapy, and breathing exercises to help mothers experience the birth of their babies with a minimum of pain and little or no medical intervention.

In Robin's case, the doctor had said, "Oh, well, I think you're going to want something to ease the pain. We'll just give you a few whiffs of ether to get you through."

So instead of being present for the birth of her son, Kate remembered nothing about it, and woke up vomiting from the ether.

Two years later, when Nora was born, someone had come up with something called saddle block anesthesia, and the doctor injected it in the nerves along Kate's spine. She was alert and conscious, aware of the satisfying sensation of the baby slipping easily from her body. But within twenty-four hours, she had developed an incapacitating headache that lasted five days. No one had told her that after a saddle block, she had to lie flat for twenty-four hours. Instead, the nurses had allowed her to get up and take a shower.

She looked down at Nora, who had stopped sucking. Her eyes were wide. She looked not a bit sleepy, just lay in Kate's arms, staring expectantly. Kate sighed and got up to warm a bottle.

———

When Mark got home from the university for a quick dinner before catching his ride to the auto plant, he picked Robin up and tickled his tummy.

"Daddy, stop!" Robin giggled.

"Hey buddy, I hear you went for a ride in an ambulance. Were the sirens going and the big red lights flashing?"

Robin nodded solemnly.

"Do you know why they did that?"

The little boy shook his head.

"It's because you're very important and the ambulance driver wanted to get you to the hospital as fast as possible so the doctors could make you all well."

"All well now, see?" He held Mark's hand against his forehead "No more tempater!"

Mark set Robin down. "Well, he seems none the worse." He put his arms around Kate. "But how about you? Are you okay?"

"I'm fine now. It was pretty scary, but Earl and Jerry were great to help like they did."

"Yeah. Tennessee diamonds in the rough, so to speak." He grinned.

"Shush, they'll hear you. But don't put them down. They're good people."

"Hey, I was only joking. I'm sure Earl's a good guy. Maybe a bit of a temper."

"I know. That banging on the walls. He told me he lost his job, so maybe it's worries and stress that get to him."

Kate had been ladling out bowls of stew while they talked, and now she set them on the table along with a basket of rolls, and lifted Robin into his youth chair. Mark devoured his food while she told him about Jerry looking so frail and tired.

"I wondered if she's sick, but I didn't like to ask. I just wish there were some way I could pay them back for their help yesterday and today."

Mark shrugged. "I don't know. Bake them a cake?" He had finished his dinner. "Sorry, I've got to run."

Kate handed him the brown bag of sandwiches she'd made. He brushed her cheek with a kiss, tousled Robin's hair, and was out the door.

Kate sat there sipping the last of her coffee, mildly annoyed about Mark's lack of interest in showing their gratitude to Jerry and Earl. Maybe he had more important things on his mind. Maybe Amanda.

She sighed and got up to clear the dishes before putting the children to bed. If she was lucky, she'd have a couple of hours of peace and quiet before she had to feed Nora again, and then fall into bed.

She thought again about Earl and Jerry. Maybe she should call Sue. They'd become good friends since they met here in Willow Run Village. Sue, with her ready laugh and refusal to let anything get her down, and her down-to-earth practical approach to life. Kate had felt comfortable with her from the first minute, as if they'd known each other forever. She always felt better after she talked to Sue.

Mark and Sue's husband Hal—Dr. Hal Sayers--had met during the war. He and Mark had met up again when they both arrived in Michigan, where Hal was doing his residency at the local hospital in Ypsilanti.

Hal and Sue and their five children, including a pair of twins, lived only two streets away in Willow Run. Kate and Mark got together with them for a potluck dinner now and then, whenever Hal wasn't too exhausted to stay awake, but Kate and Sue often met at the swings in the field behind Kate's unit, or went for walks with the children.

With sudden resolve, Kate picked up the phone and dialed Sue's number.

"Sue, it's Kate. How's everyone there?

"Oh, fine. The usual chaos when you have five kids under five, one's got a cold, and you know the other four are going to come down with it too —one at a time!"

Kate pictured Sue's round face with its usual smile, though right now she was probably frowning and patting down her dark curls, trying to smooth the unruly cowlick that stuck up on the crown of her head.

"I don't know how you do it. I can barely manage with two. Do you think we'll ever get enough sleep again?"

"Maybe when they get to college."

"Listen, Sue, I need to ask you something. Our neighbor next door—I don't think you know her. Her name is Jerry—Jerry Homan—and she took care of Nora yesterday when I had to take Robin to the ER. I think…"

"You *what*?" Sue interrupted.

"He was having convulsions. I was terrified." She went on to tell Sue about how Earl and Jerry had helped her, and how she wished she could do something to thank them.

"I asked Mark and he said, 'Bake a cake,' but that doesn't seem like much of a thank-you."

"Oh gosh, let's see." There was a pause. "You obviously can't give them money. Maybe a gift? Or maybe they'd be insulted. It's hard, when you don't really know someone that well. Maybe you just have to wait till an opportunity comes along."

"Of course. You're right. I'll keep my eye out. Thanks, Sue, And good luck with that cold making the rounds."

Kate hung up, relieved. As usual, it had helped to share her problems with Sue.

CHAPTER THREE

THE FOLLOWING SATURDAY WAS THE BIG FOOTBALL GAME WITH MICHIGAN State. All the husbands had season tickets to the university games, included in the activities fee paid under the GI Bill as part of their tuition. Mark and three of the other graduate students pooled their four tickets so that two couples could attend each game while the other two couples baby sat all the children. It was Kate and Mark's turn to go, and Mark miraculously didn't have to work the Saturday night shift—AND he was going to take Saturday afternoon and night off from studying.

Kate looked forward to the football Saturdays with Mark, although she wasn't particularly interested in the game. Big burly men spending the afternoon knocking each other to the usually frozen ground, was not her idea of an entertaining spectator sport. Even though the snow had melted this week and the sun shone brightly, the air was frigid and the wind chilling. Kate had bundled herself up in as many warm layers as she could find, fortified herself with a thermos of hot coffee, and tried to lose herself in the bright colors of the crowd, the autumn smell of smoke in the air, and the amazing energy of the cheerleaders leaping up and down, bare-legged and smiling in their jaunty blue and gold outfits. It was incomprehensible to Kate that they weren't freezing to death while she sat there in her nest of woolens, drinking hot coffee, and shivering.

Early this afternoon, they had all piled into their neighbors John and Annie's car, one of the few couples who owned one. Kate snuggled up against Mark. She'd managed to put the minor disappointment of Mark's attitude about Jerry and Earl behind her without their really talking about it again. That's so typical of our life, thought Kate. There's never any time to just sit and talk without the kids around, or one or both of us so tired all we can think about is getting some sleep. So we let things slide, hoping they'll go away. Not like when they were first married, and before the kids were born, when they had all the time in the world to sit and talk.

A memory came, unbidden, of one of those days, when they'd rented a sailboat for an afternoon and gone sailing on the nearby river. It was a rare Indian summer day in October, with the sun gentle on their backs and just enough wind to fill the sail. They hadn't talked much, but Kate remembered being as relaxed and happy as she'd ever been in her life, content in the knowledge that she loved and was loved by this man with whom she could share her innermost thoughts and know she'd be understood.

She sighed, laying her face against Mark's rough wool-clad shoulder and wondering how she could recapture that shared intimacy.

She had worried a little about leaving Robin, but he'd seemed fine after his seizures earlier in the week. She's watched him carefully, but the fever had not returned, and he was his usual energetic self, zooming his trucks around the floor or chasing a rubber ball, rolling it from room to room. In self-defense and to spare the furniture, Kate had banned throwing or bouncing indoors.

Nora wouldn't be a problem. She was a good baby, happy as long as someone popped a bottle into her mouth and changed her diaper occasionally.

The day had started out sunny, but now the sky clouded over and the cold wind picked up. Kate tried to get excited about the game and jumped up with the rest to cheer when their team made a touchdown, but her heart wasn't in it.

The huge oval bowl of the stadium was lined with thousands of cheering fans, a tapestry of blue and gold on the University side, green and white on the Michigan State side. Many of the spectators seemed oblivious of the frigid temperature and were laughing and calling out to friends. At one point someone called Mark's name, and Kate turned to look. A young woman in a beaver coat and matching hat was waving and smiling in their direction.

"Isn't that Amanda What's-her-name, the one in your class?" she asked.

"Yeah, that's Amanda. Amanda Kittering." Mark was smiling and waving back.

So here was Amanda again.

"You two seem pretty friendly," she said to Mark.

"We're in a study group together. Working on a project with a couple other guys." His eyes were on the ball as it sailed into the air in a long pass.

"Well, I think she acts much too interested in you."

Mark pretended not to hear, and instead jumped up yelling as their team scored the winning touchdown.

Kate shivered. She was glad the game was over. At least Michigan had won.

Later that night in bed, Kate tossed restlessly, dreaming of ambulances driven by enormous football players, Emergency Room nurses dressed in short skirts and waving big blue and gold pompoms, and Mark frowning at her and walking away across the football field, disappearing into the crowd. She woke up in a panic and turned over to run her hand along his back, reassuring herself that he was still there. He was asleep and didn't stir.

Nora woke at 2:00 A.M., wanting to be fed. Kate heard the sudden infant-wail, and still half asleep, she slid out of bed. The floor was freezing under her bare feet, and she felt around with a toe until she found her fuzzy slippers. She slipped them on and hurried to pick Nora up before she could wake Robin.

Nursing the baby on the living room couch, a warm afghan wrapped around both of them, Kate turned over in her mind the way Mark had been acting lately. His lack of interest in showing their gratitude to Earl and Jerry, his evasiveness when it came to Amanda. Where was the Mark she thought she knew?

She shifted Nora to the other breast, closed her eyes and tried to relax. Morning would be here all too soon.

CHAPTER FOUR

ON MONDAY MORNING ROBIN'S VOICE WOKE HER AT SIX. "MOMMY? Mommy! Me get up now!"

As Kate got out of bed feeling like a zombie, Mark stirred, then threw off the covers and headed for the bathroom with a mumbled "Good morning." Kate hoped he'd remember not to use up all the hot water. Their only supply came from a hot plate he'd illegally wired to the bottom of the water tank in a corner of the kitchen. The water fed into the bathroom shower and to the kitchen sink, but the hot water didn't go very far with four people bathing and a sink full of dishes to wash. Not to mention Nora's diapers.

At least the sun was out today. Michigan winters were bleak, and even in November, most days were cold and gray. The sun shining through the kitchen window was a welcome gift. While the coffee perked on the two-burner hot plate that served as the stove when Kate didn't have the energy to haul in wood, she packed a lunch for Mark and fixed breakfast. She had just time to grab a piece of toast and pour herself a cup of coffee when Nora woke again. By now Mark had eaten a quick bowl of cereal and after grabbing his knapsack, gave her a peck on the cheek and hurried out the door to catch his bus.

By mid-morning Kate had both children bathed and dressed and her chores done: breakfast dishes cleared away, wood brought in and piled by the stove, Nora's diapers washed in the bathroom basin and hung on lines strung across the bedroom ceiling, toys picked up with Robin's help, and herself ready for the day in dungarees and a sweater. She bundled up both children and put on her coat, then hesitated on the front stoop, shivering in the wind. Maybe she could take Danny too. Robin would like that.

She knocked on Earl and Jerry's door, calling "Hi, it's Kate."

Earl opened it immediately.

"I'm going over to my neighbor's—Annie, she lives next door to me— and I thought Danny might come along and play with Robin. Do you think Jerry would mind?"

Earl looked surprised, but he said, "No, don't think she would. She's layin' down right now." He shook his head. "But we ain't shoving off another kid on you. You got enough already."

"It's no trouble. I'm just going over for coffee. I'll have him back by lunchtime."

Right then Danny appeared, peeking around his father's legs. Kate smiled down at him. "Would you like to come play with Robin, Danny?"

Danny looked at his father doubtfully, but Kate spoke up again. "Let me take him. Remember that thing about being neighborly? Besides, it'll keep Robin happy while Annie and I visit."

Earl looked at Danny and back at Kate. "Yeah, I guess it's okay. If you're sure it's all right with your friend." He looked at her sideways. "Never met her myself."

It was true, Kate thought. The university, without adequate housing for all the married students arriving on campus, had leased apartments for many of them in Willow Run Village. The student families lived cheek by jowl with the auto workers, but there was little interaction. Most university people went about their daily lives and their social get-togethers enclosed in their own academic world, unconscious of the Earls and Jerries living amongst them. Annie and John had quite possibly never even noticed that Earl and Jerry existed.

"You should meet her sometime, and her husband John too."

Earl gave her a sardonic look, and she realized he was probably thinking how unlikely that was. He was probably right.

She took Danny's hand with a "See you later" to Earl.

Annie had the coffee pot on when they got there, and the two women sat down at the table, Nora in Kate's lap, while the little boys played on the rug. Annie's two boys were already in school, one in the cooperative nursery school at the Community Center and one in kindergarten. On days like this, she had several hours of freedom that Kate often envied.

She couldn't help envying Annie's apartment too. John had been an officer during the war and Annie had lived on Army bases until John went overseas. She had brought some of the nicer pieces of furniture she'd acquired to Willow Run. In the living room a braided rug, hand-me down from her mother, covered the plywood floor, its rich colors masking any hint of coal dust. Not that Annie had to worry about coal dust. She and John had bought an electric space heater for the living room and had the coal stove carted away. Annie had picked up some of the colors of the rug in the flowered drapes and slipcovers she'd made and had painted the walls deep green. A coat of gleaming white paint hid the ugly brown woodwork. The effect was a new clean look that had nothing to do with what most of these wartime housing units were like.

Not for the first time, Kate mentally compared her own apartment with Annie's, picturing the institutional tan walls, the bare floors, and the uncomfortable government- issue furniture. One of these days she was going to do something about that. When she had time. And the money. And wasn't so tired. She smiled wryly to herself. At least she could dream.

Her attention was drawn back to Danny. He was older than Robin—almost five, but built like Jerry, slender and small for his age, and shy. None of Earl's barrel chest and powerful forearms.

At first Danny had hung back, looking uncertainly at Kate, his eyes, a deep intensive blue like Earl's, questioning. But when Annie spilled out a box of blocks on the floor, Danny watched as Robin piled blocks on top of each other, and soon he too started to build his own tower. They played side by side, absorbed in what they were doing, until Robin added one block too many and the tower crashed to the floor. For a moment Danny looked frightened, but Robin began giggling so Danny too toppled his tower and joined in the laughter.

Annie already knew about Robin's convulsions, and Earl's rescue and the trip to the hospital. Kate had filled her in while they huddled together at the football game. As Kate sipped her coffee, she told Annie about her concern for Jerry.

"I feel so sorry for them. They're worried about money, and I think Jerry might not be well. I wish I could do something to pay them back."

"Like what?" Annie asked.

"I don't know. Just something."

"Kate, they aren't like us. Who knows what hillbillies like them like or want? We don't even know what they eat. Corn pone and greens? Or is that the Deep South?" She shrugged. "Maybe hillbillies prefer something else. Who knows?"

Kate was shocked. "Annie! They're people, same as us. I can't believe you just said that. And after they both helped me out the way they did."

"I'm sorry, but I just don't see us getting involved with people like that. Surely they have their own friends?"

"Maybe. But I've never seen anyone go in there, no friends or visitors or anything. They seem pretty alone."

Annie shrugged. "Well, I've got enough on my hands without worrying about people I don't even know."

She started talking about the ceramics class that was starting nights at the Community Center and how she planned to sign up, since John would be home with the two boys.

Kate listened politely, but after a while she got up. "It's time for Robin's lunch, so I'll be going. Thanks for the coffee."

She hoisted Nora up on her hip and hustled Robin and Danny out the door, feeling what? Irritated? Betrayed? Disillusioned? All those, and a lonely sense of isolation, of alienation from someone she had considered a friend. How could she and Annie be so far apart in their thinking?

After she dropped Danny off with Earl, her thoughts turned to an interview with Illinois Governor Adlai Stevenson she'd heard that morning on their small clock radio. Asked about the possibility of running for president the following year, he insisted he was not a candidate, though Kate thought he'd be an outstanding one: thoughtful, intelligent, and witty, his ideas expressed in calm, measured words. The country could use a man like Stevenson right then.

Kate had grown up in a comfortable home in Connecticut, with an older brother and younger sister. Both her parents had been fairly conservative Republicans, until Hoover became president, the stock market crashed, and the Great Depression hit. Kate didn't remember much about those years. Unlike so many others, her father had continued to receive his salary, though it was somewhat reduced. But she did remember how concerned her parents had been about the long lines at the soup kitchens, the suffering of suddenly homeless families, and the shocking suicides of desperate businessmen leaping to their deaths from tall buildings in New York City. When Franklin Roosevelt was elected president, both her father and mother voted for him, and from then on, they became increasingly liberal Democrats. No doubt their attitudes had influenced her own, which certainly didn't seem in tune with Annie's.

Kate's musings had carried her right through lunch as she automatically made peanut butter sandwiches and poured milk for herself and Robin, then nursed Nora, put the two children down for naps, and settled herself on the couch for a much-needed rest herself.

———

The next Sunday Kate made their special Sunday breakfast of pancakes and the rare treat of bacon. Mark had studied all day Saturday, so she hoped today he'd have some time to spend with her and the children. Right after breakfast she wrestled with the wood stove until she had a steady fire going, then started a pot roast for their mid-day Sunday meal. It could cook while she and the children went to the church service at the Community Center and Mark studied at home. With Robin in Sunday School and Nora in the nursery, Kate could enjoy some time with adults and a sermon that engaged her mind, a respite from baby and child care and conversations centered around both.

Kate hurried the children toward the Community Center, anxious to get out of the biting wind that whipped across the fields of dead weeds, scattering bits of paper and plastic trash before it. A vision of green grass and flowers, of neat white houses and fences with climbing roses, floated through her head. Would she and Mark ever get away from these dreary surroundings? Ever have enough money for a house like that?

After depositing Robin and Nora in Sunday School and nursery, Kate sat down in the big meeting hall that was converted to a church on Sunday. A portable podium stood in the front of the room, flanked by two vases of white lilies. Streaks of sunshine filtered through the high windows, illuminating the plain wooden chairs and the faces of congregants already seated. People around her nodded and smiled as Kate reached for a hymnbook and the pianist began to play. She was not very religious; she attended church for the music and for the hour of escape it afforded. Now, she felt herself relax and unwind, settling into a peaceful place as she prepared to lose herself in the music and in the words from Rev. Simpson. A slender, earnest young man, who instead of a robe wore a gray suit and tie, his sermons were usually thought-provoking, with quotes from literature and philosophy as often as from the Bible.

But today his subject was about leading a worthwhile life, based on the prophet Micah's words: "And what doth the Lord require of thee but to do justly, to love mercy, and to walk humbly with thy God." Good words to live by, thought Kate, whether you believe in God or not.

After church, Kate collected the children and trudged the path across the fields, pushing Nora in the carriage with Robin hanging on. Back at home, she began to set the table.

"Dinner will be ready in half an hour," she called to Mark, studying in the bedroom.

He emerged carrying his books. "I was just going to leave you a note. I have to go back to the university this afternoon. My study group is meeting in the library to work on that project we've got going." He busied himself with getting on his parka.

"But I've made a pot roast," Kate protested. "And you were gone all day yesterday too." Tears filled her eyes.

"I'm sorry. I wasn't planning to go, but one of the guys called and said it was the only time this week that everyone could get together, so I said I'd come." He put his arm around her shoulders. "Save me some dinner, honey. I'll be back by seven."

He kissed Nora and tweaked Robin's nose. "Bye, son. See you later."

Kate stared at the door after he'd gone. She pictured the study group, gathered around the library table, heads together, conversation flowing. She knew some of them, but one in particular came to mind. Seductive, green-eyed Amanda.

As she dished out meat and vegetables for Robin and herself, the image of Amanda stayed with her. So smart, so good looking, so not-married. So available. She pushed the thought away. She had to trust Mark. Or drive herself crazy.

CHAPTER FIVE

As FALL GAVE WAY TO WINTER, THE SUN DISAPPEARED FOR WEEKS AT A time, and the snow coming down seemed endless. The night before Thanksgiving, Kate read Robin his favorite book of the moment about *Mike Mulligan and His Steam Shovel,* before tucking him into bed. Later, sitting at the kitchen table, peeling chestnuts for the chicken stuffing, now and then popping a sweet smoky morsel into her mouth, she almost slashed her thumb when the wall beside her shook from a violent blow, and Earl's voice rose to a shout. "Geez, can't a man get somethin' to eat around here? Why in Sam Hill ain't dinner ready?"

Jerry's voice was an inaudible murmur in the sudden silence. Then Earl again, in a low voice that Kate could barely hear. "Oh, Christ, girl, why didn't you tell me?"

Kate wondered what Earl was referring to, and what Jerry had said to cause things to go so quiet. She remembered thinking, that time when Jerry had brought baby Nora back after Robin's stay in the hospital, that she might not be well. Maybe that's what this was about.

Things remained silent next door and Kate went back to picking out chestnut meats and thinking about her decision to try her hand at roasting a chicken in the baffling wood stove.

The next morning, she hauled in armfuls of wood and got a roaring fire going, which was probably a mistake since in the end the chicken was over-cooked and dry. The apple pie she attempted turned out better, with the crust only slightly burned. As she took it out of the oven, she remembered watching her grandmother bake mince pies every Thanksgiving, the neat little turkey cut-outs of dough arranged in a careful design across the top crust. Not much like her scorched apple pie, but at least it was not a total disaster.

"I'm almost getting the hang of this beast," she told Mark. "Sorry the chicken's so dry. Next time I'll let the fire die down a little first."

"You're doing great, Kate. And your gravy and stuffing went a long way toward improving the chicken."

Kate didn't tell him that she had gone to the considerable expense of a long-distance phone call to her mother. "So how do I make gravy?" she'd asked.

It had taken her a long time to even try to do much cooking and baking on the recalcitrant stove. Since Robin was born, she'd often gotten by with things she could cook on the hot plate—stews, soups, and hamburgers. But she'd decided it was time to get up her courage and tackle something more challenging, like the Thanksgiving chicken and apple pie. She vowed to do better at Christmas, maybe even a turkey.

Mark was still spending many Sundays at the university library, much to Kate's distress. The image of Amanda refused to go away, though she tried to push it out of her mind.

"Do you have to go *every* Sunday?" Kate had asked. "You must have finished that project by now."

"No. Not quite. But even when we're not working on a project, it helps to study together A couple of the guys are really good at seeing the big picture, and I'm better at the detailed stuff. We make a good team." He stopped. "Maybe not perfect...but we depend on each other to get us through."

He put his arm around her and pulled her close "I've got to stick with it, Kate. I've got no choice."

There was finality in his tone.

Frustrated at the seeming impossibility of getting through to Mark about her need for reassurance, Kate tried to focus instead on Christmas and the small tree she'd bought from the Boy Scouts. She brought out the boxes of tinsel and old-fashioned glass ornaments and she and Robin decorated the tree, to Robin's squeals of excitement. It reminded Kate of her father, how he always set up the tree with meticulous attention to the exact placement of lights, and how one year, with the tree almost ready to come down, one of the light cord connections sparked and the tree erupted in flames. She and her brother and sister had watched, mesmerized and afraid, as their father grabbed the stand underneath and dragged the blazing tree out to the front lawn, where it burned itself out. A scary but dramatic conclusion to Christmas.

Kate's mother had sent her a check to buy things for the children, and one Saturday when Hal was off duty and home with the children, Kate and Sue took the bus to Ann Arbor and went Christmas shopping. Jerry and Lily had offered to look after Nora and Robin any time, and Earl was home that Saturday as back-up, so Kate gratefully accepted.

At the children's clothing shop in town, Sue helped pick out a little pink dress with a lacy collar for Nora, and a pair of footed pajamas sprinkled with prancing reindeer. Their next stop was a toy store, where a teddy bear wearing a tiny red sweater caught Kate's eye. She added it to Nora's gifts, along with a mobile of shiny stars to hang over the bassinet. Robin had insisted he wanted a cowboy outfit, but Kate ruled out the gun and got a lasso instead. Mark was not on her list. They had agreed not to exchange presents that they couldn't afford.

"How do you shop for so many kids?" Kate asked Sue, as they roamed up and down the aisles.

"I buy mostly books for the older ones, and you saw the bubble stuff and clay and paints that I got today. The twins have plenty of hand-me-downs so I've ordered them a couple of things from the Sears catalogue— a toy truck for Tommy and a little baby doll for Heather." She shifted the bulging shopping bag from one hand to the other. "We have time for a coke before the bus comes. How 'bout if we stop in at the drug store? My treat."

As they sat drinking their cokes, Sue asked, "How's Mark? Still as busy as ever?"

"Yes, he is..." Kate had a sudden urge to confide her fears about

Amanda. "He's gone most of the time, either at the University or working. Even weekends." She hesitated a moment, then plunged on. "He's been in a study group to work on some project they're doing. Mark says it's got to do with marketing strategy—figuring out how to design the marketing program for a theoretical new business. They meet on Saturdays and Sundays in the library. That's bad enough, but one of the group is a woman, Amanda. I met her a couple of times, and she seemed awfully chummy with Mark. I don't trust her. She's gorgeous and smart and always THERE, and how do I compete with that?"

Sue looked at her thoughtfully. "And what does Mark say about that?"

"Not much. He doesn't want to talk about it. I don't really know that anything's going on. But still, I worry."

"Well, all I can say is, try to stop worrying about it. I tell myself that all the time, with all those cute young nurses hanging around Hal at the hospital. You just have to trust him. I'm sure Mark loves you. I've seen the way he looks at you."

Kate nodded. "I hope so. Still, it must be hard to spend your days looking at perfect Amanda, then come home to a wife who is always tired and sometimes cranky and not looking her best."

"So before he comes home, you could comb your hair and put on some lipstick and maybe a clean blouse without baby spit-up all over it." Sue took a sip of coke. "You'll look better and probably feel better too."

"I suppose you're right. We wives are supposed to dance around the kitchen with a mop in hand, as though it's actually fun doing housework, and at the same time look like we just stepped off the pages of *Vogue*." She shrugged into her jacket. "But I'll try to remember to take your advice and start doing a little fixing up before Mark gets home."

She gave Sue a hug as they stood up to leave. "I always feel better after I talk to you."

It was with fresh energy and renewed determination not to give in to the blues that Kate climbed on the bus for the trip home.

A day or so later she dug out her mother's recipes and started on Christmas cookies, buttery cut-outs of Santas, Christmas trees, and stars. As she rolled out the dough, she pictured the gorgeous array of cookies her mother used to make, some of them packed up for the mailman, the milk man, and the iceman. On an impulse, Kate arranged a plate of cookies and tapped on Jerry's door.

"I've been baking, and I brought you some Christmas cookies," she said when Jerry opened the door. "Merry Christmas!"

Jerry looked surprised, but then a faint smile crept over her face. "That's mighty nice of you, Kate. I don't normally do no Christmas baking. We used to have a neighbor back home who baked Tennessee Banana Cream Pies. She gave us one every Christmas."

Her lips parted, and she had a dreamy look, as if she could still taste the creamy sweetness of the remembered pie.

Her gaze dropped to the plate in Kate's hand. "They're too pretty to eat! But I reckon Danny and Lily won't waste no time getting to them. Thank you, Kate."

She took the plate and as she turned to go back in, she looked over her shoulder at Kate. "Merry Christmas to you too," she said softly.

On Christmas Eve Kate got Robin into his pajamas, and in the soft glow of tree lights and candles, he sat between Kate and Mark on the couch while they took turns reading "'*Twas the Night Before Christmas.*" After he hung his stocking on the bedroom doorknob, they tucked him in bed, then filled his stocking with little candies and gum, a packet of balloons, and a red ball, topped off with a chocolate Santa.

When Kate finished nursing Nora, Mark offered to do bottle duty so she could go to bed.

"Go on, I'll be there in a little bit. Go get a good sleep," he said, with a kiss on the top of her head and a little slap on her bottom.

Kate sank gratefully into a deep sleep and didn't hear a thing till morning when Nora woke at six. It was one of the best Christmas presents she could have received—a whole night's sleep.

Robin heard her getting Nora up and demanded to know if Santa had come. Kate put him off till the fragrance of coffee drifted from the kitchen, then she got him up and called Mark. He put their one Christmas record on the player that Kate had had in college, and with the familiar carols as background, they sipped coffee and watched Robin open his presents. The cowboy outfit was a big hit, and Robin galloped around the room spinning his lasso and pretending he was riding a horse.

"No lasso inside, Robin," Kate cautioned. "That's going to be an outside toy, ok?"

Robin's second best present was a record Kate's mother had sent: *Rudolph the Red-Nosed Reindeer*, with a little toy Rudolph that rode around in the center of the revolving record. With Robin's eyes glued on Rudolph as he watched, entranced, Kate picked up the cards she'd been saving to open with Mark. When she looked at the first one, something fell out and she caught her breath.

"Oh, my goodness! Mark, you won't believe…look at this!"

The card was from her grandmother and it included a generous check. For a refrigerator, said the note.

A refrigerator! She and Mark looked at each other in disbelief. No more emptying the pan under the ice box every night? Or having it over-flow when they forgot, sending evil-looking waves of smelly brown water over the kitchen floor? No more having to buy ice when the ice man came around every couple of days? It was almost too good to be true.

The roast turkey for Christmas dinner was more successful than the Thanksgiving chicken. It came out of the cavernous oven golden brown and crackly and deliciously moist inside. After the remains of the turkey had been stowed in the ice box and Robin had chosen three Christmas cookies for dessert, Kate relaxed on the couch, content, with her head in Mark's lap, savoring the gift of his presence the whole day. A recording of Beethoven's Pastoral filled the room—a present from Mark in spite of their agreement.

In the warm afterglow of Christmas, Kate let go of all thoughts of Amanda.

CHAPTER SIX

AFTER CHRISTMAS, THE WINTER DAYS PASSED SLOWLY, AND KATE HAD bouts of cabin fever, when the heavy gray skies seemed to press down on her and she longed to be outside. She missed the morning coffees, but when Annie suggested coming over, Kate found excuses. She wasn't over her disillusionment with Annie. Sometimes she walked the snowy sidewalks to Sue's, but most of the time they were both too busy just surviving, shoveling coal and snow, grocery shopping, doing laundry, cooking and cleaning, trying to keep their apartments warm, all those dreary chores while still finding time to keep the children entertained.

One morning a big delivery truck pulled up in front of the door. The day after Christmas, Kate had gotten out the Sears catalog and leafed through the appliance section. While Mark ate his dinner that evening, she'd shown him the refrigerator she'd picked. It included two trays for freezing ice cubes.

"Imagine, Mark, instant ice cubes for our iced tea next summer!" She stopped for a moment, savoring the thought. "And it's the right price. I'll order it first thing tomorrow, okay?"

Mark examined the pictured refrigerator. "Looks good to me. Go for it!"

So now, two burly men came tramping up to the front steps, pulling a trolley with the refrigerator, wrapped in burlap, balanced on top. They set it down in a corner while they carried out the old ice box. With the new refrigerator plugged in, humming its reassuring song, and ice cubes freezing in the trays, Kate stood there, admiring its snowy perfection. The smelly tray under the old ice box was relegated to memory.

She was still awake when Mark came home from work that night. He got in beside her and they lay in bed, listening to the beautiful hum of the refrigerator, miraculously keeping their food cold with no assistance from them or the ice man.

The next evening the snow began falling as Kate was putting the children to bed. When Mark came in, she was drowsily aware of him stomping the snow from his boots in the kitchen. Sure enough, the next morning telltale puddles had pooled on the floor. On her knees, blotting up the water with a towel, she heard Mark outside, shoveling snow off the front steps, saving her from one more chore to add to the list. All was forgiven.

Later in the afternoon, while Nora was napping, Kate took Robin out to throw snowballs and make angels in the snow. As they lay side by side, waving their arms up and down, Kate began to laugh at the memory of the previous winter, when they'd had a blizzard and the roads were closed. With the husbands stuck at home, Sue and Hal had pulled their children on a sled through the thick flakes of falling snow, to Kate and Mark's for cocoa and cookies. Sue had been pregnant with the twins, and the two men had taken the children outside and rolled a big fat snowball with a bulge in front to create a pregnant snow lady. To Sue's pretended outrage, they traced her name on the snow lady's belly.

Still smiling, Kate pulled Robin to his feet. By now the sky had cleared. The sun came out, low on the horizon, sending waves of warm orange light across the world.

"Oh Robin, look!" Kate cried. "Look at the sunset. It's like we're inside a giant Jack-o-lantern, with the sky and the snow and the houses all orange!"

Robin stared up at the sky, intrigued by this fanciful notion. But already the sky was fading, and Robin's nose was turning red with the cold.

Together they went back inside and Kate warmed milk for hot cocoa while they waited for Mark to come home.

But Mark didn't come home. Kate fed the children and put them to bed, then cleaned up their supper dishes and put hers and Mark's food in the oven to keep warm, wondering uneasily where Mark could be. She was sitting on the couch folding diapers when the phone rang. She sprang up to answer it, hoping it was Mark.

"Hello, Kate? This is Stu." One of the men in Mark's study group.

Kate felt a stab of fear. "Stu! Is anything wrong?"

"No, not really. It's just that Mark asked me to call you. He got delayed and had to go straight to work instead of coming home. He said he was sorry."

"He couldn't call me himself?" Kate asked.

"His ride was here, and he didn't have time. I was just coming out of Rackham so he yelled to me to call you."

Kate was relieved that Mark was all right, but still… "Who did he get a ride with?" she asked.

"Someone in the study group, I guess. Couldn't really see." He was talking fast. "Sorry, Kate, I've got another class and I'm running late." He hung up.

Someone in the study group? There was only Stu, someone named Fred, another man named Harvey, Amanda and Mark. Stu had a car; she didn't know about Harvey or Fred. She had a sudden, heart-stabbing conviction that it was Amanda. Had Mark missed the bus because he was with Amanda? And now she was driving him to work? Maybe he didn't really go to work, and they were somewhere together right this minute.

Kate felt the blood pulsing through her temples, and a queasiness rising in her stomach. She fell into a dark place of imagining life without Mark, a place where she was sad and alone and scared. What if he didn't love her anymore?

She got up and took the pile of diapers into the children's room, trying to shake away such an intolerable thought. Robin was scrunched up with his knees bent under him and his little butt sticking up in the air. Nora was lying on her stomach, sleeping peacefully, her thumb in her mouth. Kate gently removed the thumb and Nora gave a little sigh but didn't wake up.

Looking down at their sleeping faces, Kate felt a stirring of anger. How could Mark even begin to think about betraying this family of theirs?

She tried hard to stay awake until Mark came home, but exhaustion overcame her, and she didn't hear him come in. The next morning when he emerged from the bedroom, she faced him.

"Stu called last night. What happened that you couldn't come home for dinner?"

Mark dropped his knapsack on the floor beside his chair and sat down before he answered. "I got held up after class and missed the bus. Had to find a ride straight to the plant."

He picked up his spoon and began to eat his cereal.

Kate's voice rose. "So who gave you a ride? Was it Amanda?"

"Yes, it was Amanda. She offered, and it was the only way I was going to get to work. End of story."

He gulped his coffee and got up.

"I don't think it's the end of the story. I think there's a lot more to it." Kate was choking back tears by now.

"Oh, Kate." Mark sounded tired. "Please don't let's get into this right now." He picked up his knapsack and grabbed his jacket. "I'll see you tonight."

Kate was left with unanswered questions hanging in the air and the hopeless feeling that she had no idea what Mark was thinking.

CHAPTER SEVEN

K<small>ATE CONTINUED TO SEETHE INWARDLY ABOUT</small> M<small>ARK AND</small> A<small>MANDA, BUT</small> he turned aside her questions and refused to talk about it. It was a relief when on a wintry Saturday Kate's neighbor Marge called and invited Kate to come for coffee "and bring the children."

Marge and her husband Jake, an engineering student, lived across the street. They had no children, and Marge worked in town as a secretary in the graduate school office. Stocky, short, her brown hair tied carelessly back in a ponytail, she had grown up in a tough Detroit neighborhood and took no nonsense from anyone, including Jake. With his bristly blond hair and eyeglasses, Jake looked like a college professor, until he opened his mouth and showed the two missing front teeth that got knocked out in a fight in high school. He said he hadn't bothered yet to get them replaced, but Kate knew that, like the rest of them, money was tight for him and Marge. He probably couldn't afford to get them fixed.

Jake and Marge had gone together in high school and he was as tough as she was. In summer, when the windows were open, Kate could sometimes hear them shouting at each other from clear across the street. She thought Jake sounded like an Army drill sergeant, with a vocabulary to match, but the shouting didn't seem to faze Marge.

"I keep Jake in line with a good dose of sex whenever he behaves himself," she had told Katie with her hearty laugh. "Positive reinforcement, as they say."

Kate had a sudden thought. "Could I invite my neighbor, Jerry, to come too? I don't know if you've met her, but I bet she's as stir crazy as the rest of us by now."

"Sure, bring her along. I'd like to meet her."

As soon as she hung up, Kate called Jerry. "It's nothing fancy, just you and me and Marge for a cup of coffee," she said.

Jerry hung back at first, but when Earl overheard them talking, he said she should go.

Kate had just stepped outside when Jerry emerged from next door. She was huddled into an orange plaid wool coat, with her hands tucked under her arms.

"Jerry, how are you doing?"

Jerry had her usual half-scared look. "I'm all right," she said. She looked back at the door behind her, as if wishing she were on the other side.

"I'm glad we're going over to Marge's," Kate said. "I don't mind a little change of scenery after being cooped up all winter. How about you?"

"I guess so. Can I carry the baby for you?"

"Oh, that's all right, thanks, I've got her." Jerry looked too fragile to be carrying Nora, even just across the street. "But could you take Robin's hand?"

As they picked their way through the snow and slush, Marge, in her usual dungarees and sweatshirt, saw them coming and opened the door.

"Come on in and I'll get the door shut. This confounded everlasting wind is driving me nuts."

She took their coats and set out mugs of coffee and a plate of muffins. Jerry held out her arms for Nora and sat rocking her back and forth as if clinging to the baby for security.

"You're a natural with Nora," Kate said. "You must like babies!"

Jerry gave a small smile. "Yes, ma'am, I mean Kate. I do. I wish I'd a had more, but the doctor said I couldn't after Danny." She reached for her mug and took a sip of coffee.

"Well, at least you got one of each, a boy and a girl," said Marge. "Me and Jake both come from big families and we're gonna go it alone for a while without kids. Maybe later we'll do it, before we get too old or forget how to make babies." She grinned at Jerry, who smiled uncertainly back.

Marge turned to Kate. "You still going to that church service at the Community Center, the nondenominational one? I keep thinking I'll give it a go but I'm out of the habit. Got enough of the Catholic treatment drummed into me, growing up in Detroit."

"I go almost every Sunday, while Mark is studying. The kids go too, to the Sunday school and nursery. It's kind of a nice break, having that peaceful hour every week and something to think about besides strained carrots and dirty diapers."

"How about you, Jerry?" Marge said. "Do you have a church you go to?"

Jerry shook her head. "No ma'am. Not here. I did back home."

Marge held up her hand. "Jerry, please...it's Marge. Where was 'back home'?"

"In Tennessee, where me and Earl come from."

"Would you like to go to church with me next Sunday?" Kate asked. "See how you like it? You must miss your church and your friends."

"There you are," said Marge. "A church right here in Willow Run Village. You could go try it out."

"Well, I don't know." Jerry knitted her brows. "I'd have to ask Earl."

"At the risk of getting myself in trouble with what Jake says is my big mouth—why do you have to ask Earl?" She grinned at Jerry again, softening her words with a pat on the shoulder as she got up to pour more coffee.

"Why don't you talk to him about it when you go home?" Kate interposed quickly. "You could bring Lily and Danny too if you like."

Jerry looked at Marge and back at Kate, who nodded encouragingly. "I guess I could. Go to church, I mean. Earl would prob'ly be glad to have us out from under his feet for a while."

"Good! We can walk over together. I'll knock Sunday morning when I'm ready to go."

The three women continued to chat until Kate got up and picked up

Robin's jacket. "Miss Nora is going to have to eat any minute, so we should be going. Thanks for the coffee, Marge."

Jerry got up too and handed Nora to Kate while she put on her coat. "I thank you too, uh, Marge. It was right neighborly of you to invite me."

"Well, that's what it's all about. Being good neighbors. Kate's told me all about how you and Earl helped her out." Marge held the door open and gave Jerry another friendly slap on the shoulder as she left. "So long, you two. See you later!"

CHAPTER EIGHT

THE FOLLOWING SUNDAY KATE KNOCKED ON JERRY'S DOOR. "IT'S TIME TO go, Jerry. Are you ready?"

Earl opened the door. "I been tryin' to hurry her along but she's slower'n molasses." He shrugged. "I'll carry y'all on over and then come back for her 'n Lily. Can't fit y'all in at once anyways."

He helped Kate and the children into his truck. "Sorry my heater's busted, but it's still better'n walkin' in this weather."

It was only a fifteen-minute walk to the Community Center, but Kate was grateful for the ride, with clouds banked low overhead and the usual cold wind blowing. She took the two little boys downstairs to the Sunday School and got Nora settled in the nursery, and when Earl came back, she and Jerry sat down in the big meeting hall upstairs with twelve-year-old Lily between them.

Jerry looked around at the neat rows of folding chairs, the two urns of flowers, the candles in front of the podium, the choir in their deep blue robes.

"We didn't have no flowers or candles in our church back home," she confided to Kate. "And only hard benches to sit on. This is right nice." She stopped as the piano sounded a few chords of the first hymn.

The congregation stood, and Jerry's clear soprano soared, like a lyrical

43

descant, over the rest of the voices. She didn't even glance at the hymnal that Kate held.

As they sat down again, Kate leaned across Lily and whispered, "You have a beautiful voice, Jerry! Have you always sung?"

Jerry nodded. "Ever since I can remember."

Rev. Simpson's sermon was something about "Judge Not, Lest Thee Be Judged," which reminded Kate of Annie. Too bad Annie didn't attend church. She might have learned something from the Reverend about making judgments.

When they rose for the second hymn. Jerry stared at the hymnal, mute. Kate leaned over. "Jerry?" Jerry just shook her head and closed the book. Kate looked questioningly at Lily, but Lily avoided her eyes.

After the service, Rev. Simpson and some of the church members lined up outside the door, shaking hands and greeting people. Several of them commented on Jerry's singing, and how much they had enjoyed it. If they wondered why she went silent for the second hymn, no one mentioned it.

"Y'all come back soon," one woman said to Jerry.

Jerry smiled shyly. "Thank you, ma'am. That's like they say back home in Tennessee."

"Well, what do you know—Tennessee! We're practically neighbors. I'm from Alabama, right next door." She gave Jerry's hand an extra squeeze.

When Kate introduced Jerry to Rev. Simpson, he greeted her with a warm smile. "Glad to have you with us, Mrs. Homan. I hope you'll come again."

Kate was grateful for the way Jerry had been welcomed by this group of church members, many of them connected to the university. Thank goodness they weren't all like Annie.

When Earl pulled up at the curb a few moments later, he said he'd ferry Jerry, Lily and Danny home first, then come back for Kate and her children. "Hope you don't mind. Jerry don't do so good in the cold."

Kate nodded and took the children inside the vestibule to wait. Even there it was chilly. She hugged her coat around herself and Nora, thinking about how surprised she'd been by Jerry's singing, and how beautiful it was. Robin, meanwhile, entertained himself by jumping off the steps onto the vestibule floor.

When Earl came back, Kate hopped into the front seat with Robin squeezed between them, and Nora on her lap. As they headed for Raleigh Court, she told Earl about Jerry's singing. "She says she's always sung."

"Yeah, she was in the church choir back home. Sang solos sometimes. I reckon she misses it." He looked over at Kate. "The church gave the choir robes to wear, so Jerry didn't have to worry about havin' no decent Sunday clothes. Her family didn't have no money for things like that."

"Do you think she'd join our choir here? They didn't sing today because the choir director was away, but they do most Sundays."

"She'll probably say no, but I'll talk her into it. Do her good to get out some and do some singin' again".

So the next Sunday Earl again drove them to church, starting early for the before-service choir practice. Kate went along to give moral support. Earl was dropping off Lily with Nora and the two little boys later.

The choir director welcomed Jerry warmly. "People have been telling me what a lovely voice you have. We'd love to have you join us."

Jerry bobbed her head shyly, her pale face flushed with pleasure, her freckles standing out like a sprinkling of paprika.

The director handed Jerry a blue choir robe and the music they'd be rehearsing. Jerry slipped on the robe, looked down at the music, and Kate saw the color drain from her face. She frantically studied the music on the page, then glanced up at the singers on either side of her. Both nodded and smiled, and the blond one reached over to point out the opening notes. Jerry stared at them, uncomprehending.

And then the pianist began to play, and Kate could see the relief that flooded Jerry's face. She began to sing.

Was it possible Jerry couldn't read? No books to immerse herself in, no words to transport her away to far places and distant times? Not even the ability to read the labels on grocery store shelves, or the words in a hymnal? Kate couldn't imagine what that would be like.

She was still pondering this as they were leaving, when Jerry suddenly grabbed the railing along the steps outside the Community Center. Her face went a deadly white and Kate, with Nora in one arm, had to reach out and hold Jerry to keep her from falling.

"What's wrong, Jerry? Are you ill? Shall I get you a glass of water?"

"No…but I get these here spells and I got to sit down for a sec." She sank to the steps and wiped her face on her sleeve, making a feeble attempt to smile.

Kate looked at Lily. "What is she talking about? What spells?"

Lily glanced nervously at her mother. "It's her heart, ma'am. She says it feels kinda funny, like it's jumpin' around inside. She gets sorta weak and out of breath. My daddy makes her lie down till she gets over it."

"But has she seen a doctor?"

Lily flushed a little. "No, ma'am."

No doctor? Probably they couldn't afford it. Kate looked around for help, but people had hurried away, anxious to get out of the cold.

She was thankful when Earl's truck pulled up beside them and he jumped out.

"God, girl, you're lookin' like hell before breakfast." He picked Jerry up and placed her gently in the truck. Her eyes were unfocused and her breathing shallow. "Have you home quick's I can." He slid into the driver's seat. "I'll be back for all y'all," he said to Kate.

"No, we'll walk!" Kate called after him before he shoved the truck into gear and roared back toward Raleigh Court. Shivering, Kate and Lily picked their way across the field, Kate carrying Nora, and Lily with the two little boys by the hand.

"How long has your mother had these spells?" Kate asked.

"I don't know, ma'am. I guess I started noticing them about a year ago. Ma keeps telling me not to fret, but I reckon it's been getting worse."

"And she's never been to a doctor about it?"

"No, ma'am. None of us has seen a doctor since we've lived here, 'cept when Danny was born." Lily swallowed hard. She seemed on the verge of tears. Kate stopped with her questions and they walked on in silence.

"How's Jerry?" Kate asked when Earl opened the door. "She seemed really sick."

"Yeah, she's lyin' down but she says she's feelin' better."

"But Lily says she hasn't seen a doctor."

"No. We don't have no doc here." He hesitated. "Been puttin' it off. Back in Tennessee we had a clinic we could go to, but ain't one here." He looked down at his boots.

"I'm so sorry, Earl. Let me know if there's anything I can do."

Earl nodded and closed the door.

Inside the apartment, Kate shivered as little drafts of cold air licked around her feet. She picked up the poker, and prodded the fire in the coal stove, trying to bring the flickering blue flame back to life.

As a few sparks began to fly, her thoughts turned to Hal. Maybe he could help. He was a pretty unconventional doctor and didn't mind bending the rules a little. Mark had left early for another study group meeting and said he wouldn't be back till late afternoon. The atmosphere between them had been cool since the night he didn't come home for dinner, and Kate had left it that way. She didn't know how to resolve the issue of Amanda without a fight, so she'd tried to bury her anxiety and keep herself busy with the endless chores.

With both children down for naps, Kate paced restlessly around the living room, considering what to do. Should she wait and talk it over with Mark first? But with sudden resolve, she picked up the phone.

"Sue? I need to ask you something." She told Sue about Jerry's 'spell' and how concerned she was about her. "They don't have any money right now. Earl's been laid off and they can't afford a doctor. I just thought maybe there was some way Hal could help."

"Oh, he can probably figure something out. He's been away all week at a conference, but I'll talk to him when he gets home tomorrow night, okay?"

Kate felt a little better after she hung up. At least she had taken some action.

While they ate dinner that night, Kate told Mark about Jerry's illness and her call to Sue.

"I felt like I wanted to do something to help, and I thought of Hal."

She was not surprised when Mark frowned. "You could have waited and talked to me first. Hal's a busy guy." He went to the stove and helped himself to more mashed potatoes. "I'm not sure we should ask him to get involved. Or treat a patient outside the hospital, which he's not supposed to do."

"But Mark, you know Hal. He's always ready to help, and he can usually find ways to get around the rules. Like when Robin had heat rash last summer, remember? And we didn't know what it was? Hal just stopped by, looked at it and told us what to do, and that was that. Maybe he could do something like that for Jerry, don't you think?"

"I don't know. Maybe you should have kept Hal out of it and left things up to Earl."

"But Lily says this has gone on for more than a year. They can't afford a doctor, and there's no free clinic here like they had in Tennessee."

Mark stood up. "Okay, fine. Hal'll probably come up with something. But right now I've got to study for a quiz tomorrow." He picked his knapsack of books up off the floor and disappeared into the bedroom, closing the door.

Kate sat there sipping the last of her coffee, annoyed about Mark's reaction. Did he really think she couldn't do anything without consulting him first? It was true she wasn't using her brain for much these days beyond Dr. Spock and Dr. Seuss, and at their get-togethers with other student couples, she often felt left out, especially with some of the wives who were graduate students themselves, or already out working. When they started discussing lectures and exams and dissertations, or office politics, all she had to talk about were bottles and diapers. Still, that didn't mean she couldn't think for herself or act on her own.

The transition from college girl to wife and mother had been swift, and she sometimes missed her old college girl persona, who in retrospect had been so carefree. She still found herself wondering occasionally who this new Kate was. It was as though she'd slipped into someone else's clothes that didn't quite fit, but that with practice she was growing into. Trying to help Earl and Jerry was part of that growing, something this new Kate was determined to do.

She sighed and picked up her coffee cup to rinse in the sink.

CHAPTER NINE

HAL CAME OVER TWO NIGHTS LATER AND KATE TOLD HIM ABOUT JERRY, about her symptoms and her lack of money. Mark interrupted to say that they didn't want to put Hal in an awkward position, that if he couldn't help it was ok. That maybe Kate had spoken out of turn.

"No, it's all right. It's not that I don't want to help, but this sounds like it could be serious." Hal ran his hand over his prematurely thinning fair hair. "She'll probably need tests to find out what's wrong, maybe be admitted for observation. Not something I can handle here in her home."

He thought for a minute. "How about if you ask her to come over and let me have a quick look at her. I might get an idea of what's going on, and we can take it from there."

"Thanks, Hal." Kate threw a sweater around her shoulders and stepped next door. Earl answered her knock. "Anything wrong?"

Kate realized it was a little late to be making a neighborly call. "No, not at all. I just came over to tell you that our friend Hal is here visiting us, and he's a doctor at the hospital…"

The record player was blaring as usual and Earl yelled for Lily to turn it off.

"I hope you don't mind," Kate went on, in the sudden silence, "but I was telling him about Jerry's spell the other day, and about her being out of breath and all. He says he could take a quick look at her now, and maybe he can recommend something that would help. He won't charge anything," she added quickly. "He's not in private practice. He's paid by the hospital."

Earl seemed to be considering what she'd said.

"I don't mean to be butting in," Kate continued, "but I was worried about Jerry. I just wanted to help, the way you both helped me."

Earl shook his head. "She pretends she's ok, and it's true she usually gets over them spells, but she's had 'em for a while. I'd appreciate your doctor friend lookin' her over."

He turned and called, "Jerry, you decent?

Jerry emerged from the bedroom, freckles standing out on her pale face. She leaned against the wall. "What?" Her voice was shaky. "Hello, Kate."

"Kate has a doctor friend over next door, and he says he'll take a look at you," Earl said. "See if he can help with your spells."

Jerry looked frightened. "You know we can't pay him."

"You won't need to," Kate nodded reassuringly. "He just wants to get an idea of what might be wrong."

Jerry looked over at Earl. He took her arm. "Come on. We'll just go over and see what the Doc says, ok? Lily," he called, "Keep an eye on your brother."

Hal had gotten the bag with his stethoscope from the car, and after warming it in his hands for a minute, he listened to Jerry's lungs and heart. "A couple of deep breaths, now," he told her gently. Mark stood leaning against the wall, arms folded.

"I'm sorry, Jerry." Hal patted her on the shoulder. "I'm afraid this isn't something I can handle here. You need to be in the hospital, get some tests. You have something going on with your heart that needs attention." He turned to Earl.

"If it's ok with you, I'm going to call for an ambulance and send your wife to the ER for some tests. They can't turn her away, and she'll get the care she needs. You can worry about the hospital bill later."

Jerry looked uncertainly at Earl, who shrugged his shoulders. "We gotta do what the Doc says. I'll hustle up the money somehow." To Hal, he said, "That's good of you, Doc. I don't know how to thank you." He looked at Kate. "You and Mark too."

Kate smiled back. "We may not be in Tennessee, but we need to look out for each other here too."

Hal was already on the phone. "Hal Sayers here. I'm with a patient who needs an ambulance right away." While he gave the address, Jerry took hold of Earl's arm. She was pale and trembling. "But what about the kids?

"Don't worry, I'll figure it out."

The ambulance was there in minutes and the stretcher bearers, with Earl following, carried Jerry out. Lily emerged from the apartment next door just as they were putting her mother into the ambulance.

She ran to the stretcher and bent over her mother. "Ma! What's wrong?" Her voice was panicky.

Before Jerry could answer, Earl spoke soothingly. "Take it easy, girl. Your Ma's got a little problem with her heart, and the doc's sending her to the hospital to get checked out. You stay here with Danny, and I'll take you later to see her." He gave her arm a little shake, then climbed into his truck. "Go on, now. I'll be back before you know it."

Lily stood there looking forlorn while the ambulance pulled away, siren blaring, with Earl following it and Hal's car not far behind.

Kate and Mark watched them go, then Kate turned to Lily. "You're welcome to come over and stay with us if you don't want to be alone. You can sleep on the couch, and Danny can bunk in with Robin." Poor girl, she thought. She's only twelve, after all.

Lily straightened her shoulders. "That's all right, Ma'am. I'll get Danny in bed, and then I got homework to do, and anyway, Pa said he'd be home soon. But I thank you all the same." She opened the door and stepped inside.

"Well, goodnight, then. But call us if you need us."

As they went back in the house, Kate said, "I told you Hal would be able to help. He's such a good guy."

"Yeah, he is. But I still think you were asking a lot of him to come over here and look after Jerry on what is probably his one night off."

"I know. But that's Hal. He just wants to help when he can." Kate's tone was sharp, and Mark turned away without answering. They didn't say any more about it, but Kate could feel the tension between them.

Later, when they went to bed, Mark threw his arm across Kate and tried to pull her toward him, but she rolled away. "I'm tired, Mark. I just want to get some sleep before Nora wakes up again. Good night."

Mark removed his arm but didn't say anything. Kate fell into a restless sleep.

CHAPTER TEN

NURSING THE BABY EARLY NEXT MORNING, KATE TURNED OVER IN HER mind the events of last night. Where was this friction between her and Mark coming from? They'd always agreed about pretty much everything, like how to raise the children, how to spend what little money they had wisely, how education was so important, how they both liked the same kinds of books—especially memoirs and biographies—and both loved listening to Mahler. How they enjoyed being outdoors, going canoeing on the river or for hikes in the woods outside of town. Or used to before the children were born.

Remembering Mark's critical comments, she felt resentment flare up again. It wasn't as if she never consulted him. Besides, Jerry had gotten the help she needed, and Hal hadn't seemed to mind coming to look at her at all.

Later, as she rinsed baby bottles and put them in the pan of hot water to boil, Kate noticed Earl's truck parked at the curb. He must be staying home with Danny. She wondered how Jerry was doing. Pulling her coat around her, she knocked on his door, calling "Earl, it's Kate."

He opened it immediately.

"How's Jerry?" she asked.

"Don't know yet. I'm going over to the hospital soon's I can."

"So why don't you leave Danny with me? They probably won't let him see his mother anyway."

"Nah, it's okay. Danny can sit in the truck and wait."

"Oh, come on, Earl. There's no need for that. Let him come play with Robin."

After another brief hesitation, Earl agreed.

Kate was sitting on the couch that afternoon, reading to two sleepy little boys, when Earl knocked on the door. He reported that Jerry was tired but comfortable and being well looked after by the nurses. The diagnosis was atrial fibrillation.

"Doc called it A-Fib. Says it means the heart ain't working right so the blood don't get pumped fast enough. Jerry has a clot in her leg because of it." A worried frown creased Earl's forehead. "They got her on something called a blood thinner. Doc says it'll dissolve the clot."

"Well, it's good they have a diagnosis, and Hal will see that they do everything they can. I'm sure Jerry's going to be fine."

Earl nodded, though he looked doubtful. He went over and picked Danny up. "Come on, boy. Time for your nap."

"I'm making a meat loaf for dinner," Kate told him. "I'll bring some over to you and the children. And don't say no. I won't hear of it." She surprised herself at how assertive she sounded.

Earl surprised her too when he accepted with no argument. "Gee, thanks. Me and the kids love meat loaf." He left with another thank you and Kate settled Robin in bed and herself on the couch for a much-needed nap.

Earl continued to visit Jerry, and Kate offered to take care of Danny when he was gone. The two little boys played well together, and it actually helped Kate to have Robin happily engaged and needing less attention. It occurred to her that she could also provide Earl and the children with some more meals. She doubted if Lily did much cooking, and Earl probably none.

Maybe she could enlist help from some of her friends. Not Annie. Not after the conversation they'd had about Jerry and Earl. She hesitated to call Sue, figuring she was one friend who already had plenty to keep her busy.

But while they were out walking the children the day after she delivered the meat loaf, Kate mentioned it to her.

Sue stopped the double stroller she was pushing and called to her other three children, who were lagging behind. "Come on, kids. Hurry it up!"

Two-year-old Ellie's chubby legs pumped up and down as she endeavored to keep up with her brother and sister.

"Help her, you two!" Sue admonished. "Hal Junior, take her hand, and Laura, you take the other. There, that's more like it."

To Kate, she said, "Got to keep the troops under control or it's total chaos." She reached to tuck the blanket more snugly around the twins. "It's great you're helping Earl and Jerry like this. Much better than baking a cake! Hal told me about the fix they're in and I'd like to help too. How about dinner tonight? I'm making chicken with dumplings and I can easily make extra."

"I wasn't going to ask you," Kate protested. "You and Hal are doing enough already. I thought I'd call Marge and see if she'd help, and maybe Beth too."

"I bet they would. But at least I'll take tonight." She reached up to tuck her dark curls back under her red stocking cap. "Let me know if you need me to do it again."

That was so typical of Sue. No matter how busy she was, she was always ready to help someone else in a pinch. So different from Annie.

That evening Hal came to the door with a big basket on his arm. "Sue made some brownies too. Shall I just knock on Earl's door?"

"Yes, go ahead. I told him you were coming. Tell Sue thanks."

"Sure thing." As he turned to leave, Kate stopped him with a question.

"Hal, how is Jerry?"

"Coming along, actually. We've got to keep her until the clot in her leg dissolves, but with proper medication and enough rest, I think she can come home in a few days. She's always going to have to take medication and not get over tired. But she should be fine."

A few more days. That was good news. Earl would be relieved.

With a cheerful nod, Hal backed out the door, carrying the basket with the pot of chicken and the pan of brownies and refusing Kate's offer to help. Kate heard him knock on Earl's door and the rumble of voices, then the door closing as Hal left.

Marge had reacted like Sue. "Sure," she said, when Katie asked for her help. "What night?"

"How about tomorrow?"

"Count me in. I made lasagna over the weekend and there's tons left over. I'll take it across the street when I get home from work." She nodded toward Earl and Jerry's unit.

"Let me know when she gets home. I'll go over and say hello. She seems a little lost in this sea of university types."

The next day Kate, carrying Nora and taking Robin by the hand, walked down the street and knocked on the door of another friend, Beth, who had a baby a little older than Nora. When Beth opened the door, Katie once again was struck by how pretty she was, her blond hair curling around her face, her figure in black pants and white shirt model-perfect in spite of so recently giving birth. Kate sighed. She had been working on getting rid of the slight bulge in her belly ever since Nora was born.

Beth invited her in, but Kate had to get home, as it was almost lunch and nap time. She explained what had happened to Earl and Jerry and what she was doing to try to help.

"Of course I'll help. We're leaving tomorrow for an early Thanksgiving with my parents, but I made way too much spaghetti sauce for our dinner tonight. I could take them that and some pasta. I'll be back in a week, so if you still need help, let me know."

Kate hurried the children home through the swirls of snow that had suddenly begun to whip around them. At least Sue and Marge and Beth had come through. Unlike Annie, whose attitude still rankled.

She remembered with a mixture of amusement and concern how Earl had reacted when she told him either Hal or Sue would be over with dinner the night before.

"Jeez, girl, you trying to make a delivery boy outta the doc?"

She'd told him not to worry, that was just Hal, "He's like that," she said. "No pretensions."

"Pretensions, huh? Where do you get all them big words, in college?"

"Some of them, I guess. But a lot of them from reading. You don't have to go to college to learn new words."

Earl looked more uncomfortable than Kate had ever seen him. "Not everybody can read," he muttered.

Was he thinking of Jerry?

CHAPTER ELEVEN

THE THREE OF THEM, KATE, SUE AND MARGE, TOOK TURNS PROVIDING dinners for Earl and the children, but Earl refused to let them foot the bill for the extra groceries.

"They're rehiring at the plant," he said, "so I've got my old job back. You girls give me the grocery list, and your own lists too, and I'll pick the stuff up after my shift. You can pay for your own food, but you ain't going to cook for me and the kids and pay for ours too!"

True to his word, he delivered the separate orders to each one. It was a boon to Kate, as it saved her from hiking across the fields. It also meant that Marge and Sue got to meet Earl. They told Kate that he didn't have much to say at first, but after the second and third deliveries, he loosened up and started to joke with them.

"Can't have the Doc being the only delivery boy around here," he told Sue.

And when Marge thanked him for saving her the trips to the grocery store, he said, "Glad to do it in return for a bunch of smart college girls cookin' my meals."

Jerry came home the next week, and she flatly refused when Kate told her they'd continue to help out with dinners.

"I know I got to take it easy for a while," she said. "But you and your friends done enough. I thank you for it. It was a big help to me and Earl. But I got Lily to help cook—time she learned—and Earl to do the shopping. We can manage fine." She closed her eyes, exhausted, and Kate quietly left.

———

The snow gradually melted and warmer days heralded the coming of spring, As Jerry's strength returned, she went back to singing in the choir. She had no trouble learning the music. She had an ear for it, and once she heard something played, it became part of her being. The words were a different story.

After her first Sunday back in the choir, Jerry intercepted Kate as she was hauling in a bucket of coal. "Kate, um, I gotta ask you a favor." She shifted on her feet, looking uncomfortable. "I don't want to ask Lily 'cause she's busy with her schoolwork an' all. It's just that some of them hymns the choir sings ain't familiar to me. Do y'all think you could help me memorize the words?"

So without either of them acknowledging Jerry's inability to read, they sat together on Kate's couch each week while the little boys napped, and Jerry repeated the words Kate read to her, until she had them memorized.

Mark was still gone most of the time, including many Sundays. One evening the phone rang while Mark was at work at the plant, and a woman's voice asked for him.

"He's not here," Kate said, balancing Nora on one hip. "Can I take a message?" Right away she thought of Amanda. The haughty tone certainly sounded like her.

"No, never mind. I wanted him to bring a book I need, but I'm seeing him at lunchtime tomorrow anyway. Tell him our usual place." The receiver clicked.

A familiar sick feeling clutched at the pit of Kate's stomach. Their usual place? What did that mean? She and Mark had not mentioned Amanda since the night she drove him to work. Mark fell into bed exhausted most nights, and Kate was perpetually tired too. It seemed easier and maybe safer to just let the subject of Amanda go.

But now…?

The next morning at breakfast Kate said, "You had a call last night. A woman. She didn't say her name, but I wouldn't be surprised if it was your pal Amanda. She said she'd see you at the usual place for lunch today. So what's that all about?"

"Oh, yeah, it was probably Amanda." He evaded her eyes. "It's not about anything. Our group has to work on some stuff sometimes during lunch in the cafeteria."

"The way she said it, it sounded like more than a casual working lunch. What's going on?" Kate felt an overwhelming sense of betrayal.

"Nothing. Let it drop, Kate. Don't make something out of nothing." He picked up his jacket and knapsack and headed out the door, ignoring her furious "It doesn't sound like nothing!" that followed him out.

Kate grabbed a sponge and began scrubbing hard at the stains on the worn wooden drain board, trying to scrub away her anger and anguish as she imagined the possibility of Mark being unfaithful. Her tears splashed onto the soapy wooden surface, and her throat contracted in pain. She felt herself sinking once again into that same dark place of life without Mark.

Robin had stopped pushing Cheerios into his mouth and was looking at Kate with big scared eyes.

"It's all right, baby" She swallowed her tears. "Mommy's not upset any more. Daddy and I just had a little argument, but everything is all right now."

She picked him up and gave his chubby little body a hug. "Why don't you play with your blocks while I clean up the kitchen? Then we'll go for a walk with Nora, maybe go play on the swings."

As she washed the breakfast dishes, brought in more wood for the stove, and started Nora's empty bottles boiling, Kate's anguish gradually melted away, leaving her feeling unsettled, not sure what to think. She'd always believed in their wedding vows, believed that she and Mark would love and cherish each other forever, that nothing could change that. But now she was not so sure. Maybe Mark was just having a mild flirtation with Amanda. Or maybe it was more than that. Maybe love wasn't forever after all. The hollow feeling came back at the thought.

They had met six years before at a fraternity dance when Kate was a sophomore and Mark was a senior. Maybe that love-at-first-sight thing was true. Kate had spotted Mark first, his tall frame leaning against the wall on the opposite side of the room, watching the dancers. She liked his looks, not exactly handsome, but strong features, wavy brown hair cut short, and a healthy tan, as though he spent a lot of time outdoors. She looked away, embarrassed, when he caught her staring at him. But moments later, he was crossing the room toward her.

"Dance?" he asked, smiling down at her. She nodded, her throat suddenly tight. As he put his arm around her, she felt a magnetic pull. She wanted to lean close and put her cheek next to his.

"I'm Mark" he said. "Mark McIntyre."

"Kate," she managed to say.

He pulled her closer and danced toward the terrace door. "Do you mind if we go outside and get some fresh air, Kate Whoever You Are?" She nodded again. "Kate Austin," she said

Outside, Mark took her hand, and a pleasant tingle ran up her arm. They walked down the steps to a bench by the river and sat, his arm around her shoulders, and began to talk. About their childhoods, their families, his time in the Army, her growing up in Connecticut near the beach, their hopes and dreams for the future.

"I enlisted in the Army right after Pearl Harbor," Mark said. "That Sunday when we heard the news, I'd gone to the shore with a couple of friends, and on the way home we had the radio on and we were singing along to *Chattanooga Choo Choo,* when suddenly the announcer cut in with the special news bulletin about the Japanese attacking Pearl Harbor."

"I didn't know till my father turned on the radio for the six o'clock news," Kate had interjected. "We'd been putting up Christmas decorations all afternoon, with carols playing on the Victrola. I got really scared when I saw how worried my parents looked."

"I know. It seemed like the whole world had changed in a second. We didn't know what to expect next."

By the next day they knew that the Japanese had sunk the entire American Pacific fleet, and Congress declared war. Mark and his buddies signed up that same week.

"We were gung-ho to rip the hell out of the Japanese. Eighteen-year-old kids with no idea what we were getting into."

Mark had only eight weeks of basic training, learning how to fire rifles and machine guns, being lectured about how evil the enemy was, and then shipped off for further training in the Arizona desert before being sent to the North African campaign.

He shrugged. "We had to grow up fast."

His division landed on a beach in Morocco in November, 1942, and he was wounded late the first day. "I didn't realize I was hit until I looked down and saw blood pouring from my leg," he told Kate.

He was evacuated back to the States, spent several weeks in the hospital, and left with a metal pin in his leg. Luckily, during his convalescence he had been given the qualifying exam for an Army program that was recruiting qualified soldiers for accelerated training in Medicine and Engineering. Mark had done particularly well on the Aptitude Test for Engineering.

"So instead of going back to Africa, with typical Army illogic I was sent to pre-med at Northwestern—not engineering. By the time the war ended, I had completed the accelerated pre-med program and started medical school."

He dropped out as soon as he was discharged from the Army. "I never wanted to be a doctor, but the Army didn't give us a choice. I know I was lucky to be sent to school, but what I really wanted was to go back to college and major in business administration. So after the war, that's what I did."

"Why did you choose Business?" Kate had asked.

Mark said he thought a Business degree would give him all sorts of options, either in the business world, or with institutions of higher education, or maybe a non-profit.

"I wanted to do something meaningful in my life, but I also wanted to earn a good living. I thought an MBA was the way to do it."

Kate told Mark about growing up near the ocean in Connecticut, about her father being a school principal and her mother a librarian, so the house was always full of books.

"I always had my nose in a book," she confessed. "Even at the beach in summer. When I was young, my mother used to sometimes take my book away and make me go outside and play. Even though she was a librarian, she thought all that reading might be too much of a good thing."

Her father had taught her and her brother and sister to sail, but Kate was the one who loved it best. She had happy memories of sun-splashed days on the ocean, wind whipping her hair, flying over the waves with spray stinging her face.

As they talked and the hour got later, it was clear something was happening that night that would change their lives.

They were married only a few months later and moved into a small apartment near the university. Mark started graduate school while Kate continued with her classes and worked part-time at the university bookstore. She dropped out of school at the end of her junior year after she discovered she was pregnant with Robin.

In spite of having almost no money, and no idea how to take care of a baby, they'd been surprised by how ecstatic they were when Robin was born. Back in the little apartment, they'd sat watching the baby wave his arms and legs around in the air and marveled at the variety of hiccups and gurgles produced by this tiny human being. Kate remembered Mark saying with a smile, "I didn't know a newborn could be so entertaining."

Where had that closeness, and maybe that love, gone?

They'd moved to Willow Run Village when the small apartment in town became crowded with two adults, a toddler, and an expected baby. Kate hadn't been prepared for the realities of life in Willow Run, and she sometimes thought longingly of the cozy apartment in town, with its central heating, hot running water, modern gas stove, and its closeness to the university and to shops and restaurants.

She pulled herself away from memories of what her life used to be, and went about cleaning up the kitchen, getting dressed, feeding the children, and then moved through the day like an automaton. She whipped together a quick supper of grilled cheese sandwiches and tomato soup and waited for Mark to come home, uncertain what would transpire, but hoping, somehow, he could, and would, convince her that that love still existed.

But Mark came home late. The bus hadn't been on time and he had to wolf down his soup and sandwich and hurry out to work. Kate went to bed almost as soon as the children were settled and was asleep when Mark came in.

The next morning was no better. Mark overslept, in spite of Kate calling him several times, so once again he had to bolt down his cereal and take off. Kate gave up trying to talk to him and decided to wait until the weekend.

CHAPTER TWELVE

On Saturday the sun was shining, and it was actually warm enough to take the children out for a walk without snowsuits and boots. Kate strolled around the long block, savoring the sun's warmth on her face. Robin hopped along beside her, picking up a collection of "pretty stones." To Kate they just looked like loose gravel, but he was so happy with his finds that she let him fill her coat pockets. They ended their walk at the swing set in the field behind their unit, and as she pushed Robin, she studied the scrubby wasteland around her. A few scraggly weeds were making a feeble effort to put up some pale green shoots. What would it take to fence in a little area outside their back door and try to get grass to grow? Green grass! Just the thought of it made her smile. But would anything grow in this unfriendly looking soil?

That afternoon, Kate knocked on Jerry's door. "I want to ask you something," she said, when Jerry opened the door. "Did you and Earl have a lawn or garden when you lived in Tennessee?'

Jerry's thin reddish eyebrows lifted in surprise. "Well, not exactly a lawn. We had lotsa green grass round our cabin that just grew wild, but we had a garden too. Earl liked to grow tomatoes and corn and beans, and sometimes put in a few flowers."

"Do you suppose we could get some grass to grow behind our units?

We could put up a chicken wire fence and the kids could play out there, instead of on the sidewalk or trying to climb up on the coal bins." Kate's voice rose with enthusiasm. "And maybe we could have some flowers!"

Jerry's face lit up at the thought. "I reckon we could ask Earl. He wouldn't have no trouble diggin' up a patch and puttin' up a fence. He's done that plenty of times in Tennessee."

"Can you ask him tonight? And see if he knows how much it would cost. For seed and fencing and stuff. I don't know where I'd get the money, but I'll figure something out."

Jerry said she'd talk to Earl that night and let Kate know. When she closed the door, she looked happier than she had in a long time, except when she was singing.

In thinking about the prospect of green grass and gardens, Kate had tried to put aside the nagging worries about Mark. But now her somber mood returned. That night, before Mark came home from the university, she remembered Sue's advice. She had neglected to follow it, but now she went into the bathroom and washed her face, put on some lipstick, dabbed a touch of perfume behind her ears, and changed into a pretty blouse.

Mark got home early for once, and after the children were in bed, Kate sat down beside him on the couch.

"You smell good." He grinned at her. "You look good too!"

"I'm sorry I yelled at you the other morning," she said. "It's just hard, imagining you with Amanda so much of the time."

Mark looked away for a minute, then back at her, a faint flush creeping across his face.

"Stop worrying, Kate. Believe me, she's not my type." He stood up, then leaned over and kissed her. "It's been a long day and I'm bushed. I'm hitting the hay."

Kate looked after him, disappointed in his tepid response once again to her unspoken plea for reassurance. She wanted to believe him, but every time the subject of Amanda came up, he seemed evasive. It was getting harder and harder to follow Sue's advice to 'just trust him.'

She picked up Nora and held the warm little body against her, drawing comfort from the soft gurgles and sweet baby smell.

On Sunday Mark had left for the university by the time Kate was home from church. He said he was meeting with the whole study group, not just Amanda, so Kate made up her mind not to think about it. During the children's nap time, she settled on the couch and leafed through a month-old copy of *Good Housekeeping* that her mother had sent her. She wondered if this was an indication that her mother considered her a less than proficient housewife. What a term. Housewife. As though she were married to a house. On second thought, she pretty much was.

As she idly turned the pages, she came across a picture of a beautifully landscaped back yard, along with an announcement of a contest. Curious, she read the guidelines: Tell us how you would redesign your backyard if you had the money to do it, they said. Deadline April 15. First prize was one hundred dollars. Winners to be announced May 15.

Kate looked at the calendar hanging on the kitchen wall. April 10. There was still time. I can do it, she thought. Pictures of a made-over scrubby back yard unreeled in her head: the white picket fence, the flowers growing in profusion, a carpet of emerald grass. Maybe a picnic table under a bright umbrella.

She pulled a pad of paper from Mark's desk in the bedroom and began to dream, and then to write. Scribbling furiously, she described their weedy expanse of back yard, and then her vision of a transformed garden. She even made a sketch and colored it in with some of Robin's crayons. A yellow forsythia bush in one corner, a sandbox in another. The picnic table lined up near the back steps. Bright petunias along the far side of the fence, and lots of open grass for the children to play on. And as an afterthought, a plastic wading pool in the middle for hot summer days. When she finished writing, she read it over once, typed it out, then found an envelope and wrote the address. She couldn't find a stamp, so she called Marge.

"Marge, do you have a stamp I can borrow? I want to put something out for the mailman first thing tomorrow, and we're out of stamps."

"Sure thing, kiddo. I bought some just yesterday. Come on over."

Kate put the letter in the mailbox the next morning with a flush of excitement. She'd never won anything in her life, but there was a first time for everything, wasn't there?

Later in the day she saw Jerry sitting on the front steps, with Danny beside her turning the pages of a book. Kate joined them on the stoop.

"Jerry, did you say anything to Earl about maybe fixing up the back yard?"

Jerry nodded. "Yes, he said he'd help. It prob'ly won't cost much to buy some grass seed and maybe a few flowers. Earl knows someone at work who has a big garden. He might give us some of his flowers." She looked almost animated, bright-eyed, her cheeks flushed. "I had petunias in Tennessee."

Kate thought a minute. The contest results wouldn't be announced for more than a month and there wasn't much chance she'd win. Still, it wouldn't hurt to get started. She could scrape out a little from the grocery money to begin with. "Do you think Earl would have time to start digging up the yard any time soon?"

"Don't know, but I'll ask soon's he comes home."

Danny had been quietly paging through his book, and now he held it up to his mother. "What does it say about the train, Ma?"

"It says it's a mighty strong little train that's going to go right smack over the mountain." Jerry glanced at Kate as if expecting her to comment.

"Yes, Danny, look! It's *The Little Engine That Could*. It's taking Christmas toys to the children who live on the other side of the mountain. Would you like me to read it to you?"

Danny nodded. Kate turned back to the beginning and began to read. She noticed Jerry following intently, staring at the words as if trying to make sense of them. Kate kept on reading to the end of the story, then closed the book and held up the cover. "See, Danny, it says right here on the cover: *The Little Engine That Could.*" She pointed to the words as she read, then traced the letters with her finger one by one and read them out loud. T-h-e L-i-t-t-l-e E-n-g-i-n-e T-h-a-t C-o-u-l-d. "So what's this big one here, Danny?" she pointed to the capital T.

Danny shook his head. "Don't know."

"T!" Jerry whispered.

'Yes! T," Kate said. "See, Danny, once you learn all the names of the letters and what sounds they make, you can read almost any word. Some day soon you'll be able to do that, just you wait and see."

Danny stared up at her, then reached for the book, but his mother took it from Kate's hands.

70

"What's this next letter, Danny?" she asked, pointing to the h.

Danny shook his head. "It's an h, Danny," Kate said.

"An h." Jerry squinted at the book title.

"Robin has a whole book about the alphabet," Kate told Danny. "When he wakes up from his nap, I'll get it and you can borrow it."

"Okay." Danny looked only mildly interested, but Kate could see that Jerry was paying close attention.

"I'll bring the book over later," she said to Jerry.

After supper Kate knocked on Jerry's door. "Here's the book for Danny," she said. "You can borrow it for as long as you like. Robin won't even miss it. My mother just sent him a new alphabet book that's his current favorite."

As the door closed Kate heard Lily say, "Want me to read it to Danny, Ma?"

She hoped Jerry would sit there too and start learning the letters along with Danny. She's smart, Kate thought. I bet she'll be a quick study.

Earl came over after work a few days later, shovel and borrowed measuring wheel in hand. "You want to show me where you and Jerry got in mind to make this here lawn?" he asked.

By the following evening he had the whole area dug up behind their units and had marked with lime where the fence should be.

"Still too cold for planting," he told Kate. "But grass can go in soon, and I'll start lookin' into fencing." He shifted from one foot to the other. "You know," he added. "You got Jerry all fired up about this garden. That, and the singing has done her good. I gotta thank you for that. She weren't very happy here till now."

"I'm pretty excited about the garden too. It's the first one I ever had, so I'll need lots of advice from you and Jerry about what we should do."

"One thing we oughta do is get some manure. The soil here is real crap —beg your pardon, crummy. This fella at work who has the big garden keeps chickens too. He said we can have some of the manure." He chuckled. "You ever shoveled chicken shit before?"

"No. Why, do you need me to help?"

"Wouldn't hurt to have two people to make the work go faster. The stuff stinks something terrible."

"I guess I could." Kate wasn't sure what she was letting herself in for, but if it was for the garden—why not?

After Earl went back in, Kate sat on the back step, admiring the freshly turned soil, breathing in the earthy scent and imagining the garden-to-be. She thought about Earl, and how willing he was to help with the garden. In spite of his rough ways and the shouting and cursing she heard through the walls, she was pretty sure he really cared about Jerry. Maybe a lot of his seeming anger was from worrying about her being so frail, and homesick for Tennessee.

Nora was babbling in the stroller she'd graduated to, and Robin was digging happily in the dirt with his little shovel. Content, Kate stretched out her arms in the weak spring sunshine. Thoughts of Mark and Amanda came back unbidden, but with an effort of will, she held them at bay.

CHAPTER THIRTEEN

THE NEXT MORNING AT BREAKFAST, KATE TOLD MARK ABOUT EARL digging up the back yard and how she and Earl and Jerry were going to try planting grass back there. She didn't mention the contest. She didn't want to jinx her slim chances of winning by talking about it.

Mark looked doubtful. "Do you think anything will really grow in that soil? It doesn't look too promising." He got up and looked out the window. "But it would be nice to have some grass for the kids to play on. Tell Earl I'll help with watering on weekends, if he wants." He paused, with a faraway look in his eyes. "I used to sit on the front steps with my dad after dinner while he waved the hose back and forth over the lawn. I remember him saying it was important to water new grass every night."

"I'll tell Earl. He'll be glad for the help." And I'm glad there's something we don't have to argue about. And that you sound friendlier toward Earl.

"Oh, and Earl also needs help bringing back some manure from his friend's chicken coop." She made a face. "He said it smells really bad, but I said I'd do it."

Mark shook his head. "You're really into this garden thing, aren't you?" He started to laugh. "My wife shoveling chicken poop? You gotta be kidding."

73

Kate laughed too at the picture it conjured up. "But I don't have to shovel. Earl said he just needs someone to steady the buckets while he shovels, and we both know Jerry is too frail to do it. I can take Robin with me and Jerry offered to keep Nora. We're going tomorrow when Earl gets home from work."

"Doesn't sound like a lot of fun, but good luck!"

She and Mark hadn't mentioned Amanda since the night he had gone off to bed without really addressing Kate's worries. She had avoided the subject and thrown herself into plans for the garden, trying to distract herself from the disquieting thoughts that lurked in the back of her mind. Maybe she should seize this moment to bring up Amanda again, but she was beginning to feel like a nagging wife. With a sigh, she once again thrust away the troubling image of Amanda. Maybe she was too afraid of what the truth might be.

The following afternoon she and Robin climbed into Earl's truck and they drove to the friend's farm not far out of town. The sun was already setting, and Kate shivered in the chill spring air.

"Jack said to help ourselves if he wasn't around. Just not to let the chickens outta the yard."

Kate lifted Robin down from the truck, and he glued himself to the fence, entranced by the sight of chickens running around, clucking wildly at the appearance of visitors. Earl and Kate let themselves in, carefully closing the gate behind them, and began filling several big buckets with manure. Luckily it didn't take long.

"You weren't exaggerating when you said chicken manure smells!" Kate waved her hand in front of her nose to get rid of the odor as Earl lifted the heaping buckets into the truck.

Back in Willow Run, Kate collected Nora and herded Robin inside, leaving Earl spreading manure over the yard and raking it in. He had barely finished before darkness enveloped the garden.

———

Earl worked overtime at the auto plant for the next ten days while Kate tried to contain her impatience for something to happen in the backyard. He finally appeared one late afternoon with a bag of grass seed and a hose.

"We're gonna have to keep the seed moist," he told Kate. "Maybe you and Mark can handle that most of the time, and I'll help when I can." He coiled the hose up by the back step. "I got a fixture to attach to the kitchen faucet, so we can connect the hose pipe there. A little messy, maybe, but it'll work."

"A hose pipe?" Kate asked.

"It's a hose." He shrugged. "We call 'em that in Tennessee."

"So how much were the seed and the...um, hose pipe?" Kate asked, a little fearfully.

"The seed weren't much, and I been wanting to buy a hose pipe anyway. I can use it to wash my truck."

"And the seed? How much do I owe you?" Kate was counting up in her mind how much money she had left till the next month's checks arrived.

"I got five pounds to start. $4.65. We can get more if we run out."

Not too bad, Kate thought. Mark will get his week's pay from the plant on Friday, and the monthly government check by Monday.

"Is it okay if I settle with you on Friday?"

"Sure, not a problem." He slit open the bag of seed and they both took a handful and began sprinkling it around. When they were finished, Earl went inside to attach the hose and then lightly watered the scattered seed. He called Jerry to come look and they all stood admiring the patch of wet earth, the first step in making the imagined lawn a reality.

By now it was dusk and getting chilly. Kate wrapped her sweater closer and went in to relieve Lily, who had been keeping an eye on Robin and Nora.

"Thanks, Lily. We got the seed in. Your mom and dad are the greatest."

Lily rolled her eyes. "Maybe when they ain't *your* mom and dad." But she smiled when she said it.

Kate turned the radio on to get the news while she juggled cooking dinner with the hungry demands of her daughter. She'd gradually gotten the knack of banking the stove fire in the morning so that it stayed warm all day and was ready to be fired up with a little more wood when dinner time came. As soon as things were simmering on the stove, she sat down to nurse Nora. Her milk was almost gone now, and six-month-old Nora would have to be weaned soon.

A name on the news caught her attention. Adlai Stevenson. President Truman wanted him to run for the Democratic nomination for president and Stevenson was saying no. He insisted that he was not interested and would not change his mind. Too bad, thought Kate. I would have voted for him.

A day or so later, she was in the Community Center Laundromat, shoving two loads of laundry into the machines with Robin trying to help. He meant well and she appreciated his enthusiasm, but half the clothes landed on the floor so there was a lot of picking up. Nora was banging her rattle on the front of the stroller, adding to the roar and whoosh of washing machines and dryers. Kate looked at the woman using the machine beside hers and shrugged her shoulders. "Kids!" she laughed. "They think the more noise and confusion the better."

The other woman laughed too. Kate had seen her here before but didn't know her name. "I'm Kate McIntyre," she said. "I've seen you here before."

"I know. I've seen you too. My name is Barbara Braden. Nice to meet you." She began throwing her dry clothes into the laundry basket beside her, saying, "I've got to catch the bus to the university. No time to fold these now."

"You're a student?" Kate asked.

"Yes, getting my master's in political science. I'm so sorry, but I have to run." She smiled at Kate. "Next time we meet, I hope we'll have more time to talk."

When her wash was done, Kate loaded the wet clothes into a basket and set it on the wagon along with the children, Robin holding Nora tightly in front of him. It was a big load, but she couldn't afford to put two loads in the dryer. As usual, the laundry would hang on the lines strung across the bedroom.

As she pulled the wagon across the field, she thought about the woman she had just met. Barbara Braden. A political science major, like Kate herself had been. And doing graduate work, like Kate was hoping to do eventually. She felt nostalgic for those days. Unlike many of her class-mates, she'd always liked school, and was glad to go back in September in spite of how much she loved summer. Maybe some day.

CHAPTER FOURTEEN

THE NEXT TIME KATE HAULED CHILDREN AND LAUNDRY TO THE Laundromat, Barbara was there again. "You said you're a Poli Sci major?" Kate asked. "I was too, but I dropped out after my junior year when I got pregnant." Again she felt the familiar tug of nostalgia for that former world. "What do you hope to do when you graduate?"

"After my husband finishes med school here, I want to get into some kind of government work in Washington," Barbara replied. "But meanwhile I'm getting my feet wet by serving on the Democratic Town Committee. It's a challenge, finding fellow Democrats in this Republican bastion. They're scarcer than hens' teeth." She laughed, shaking her head. "Sorry, that was one of my grandmother's favorite expressions."

"Mine too! So what does the Democratic Town Committee do?"

As they tossed laundry into the machines, Barbara explained that the committee right then was focused on trying to get enough Democrats on the local ballot. In most of the county, Republicans usually ran unopposed.

"We'd like to change that. At least give them a run for their money."

She went on to say that they were also recruiting block workers who could distribute flyers before the election and help people get registered to vote, plus on election day make phone calls reminding people to vote and offering rides to the polls.

Kate was silent for a minute. I could do that, she thought. It would be at least a little something linked to what I was doing in college. And I wouldn't have to worry about a babysitter. It's all on my own block or on the phone.

"Can I volunteer to be a block worker for Raleigh Court?" she asked Barbara.

"Sure! That would be great. We don't have anyone there. Give me a call and we'll get you signed up." She handed Kate a scrap of paper with her phone number on it.

"Too bad Adlai Stevenson says he won't run," Kate said. "I like what I hear about him."

"Yes, well, that might change. A lot of people are trying to get him to reconsider, including President Truman."

When Kate got back home, she called Barbara with her address and phone number.

"Glad you called. We're having our monthly meeting at the Community Center next Tuesday, 7:00-9:00 P.M. Do you think you can make it?"

"I'll try. I'll come if I can find a sitter."

Maybe she could get Lily to come over after the children were in bed, with Jerry to back her up.

She had just hung up the phone when it started ringing again. She picked it up and heard a man's voice on the other end. "Is this Kate McIntyre?"

"Yes, this is she." She didn't recognize the voice. Some pesky person selling something she didn't need and couldn't afford. She almost hung up, but his next words stopped her.

"Mrs. McIntyre, this is Brian Kessler from the Good Housekeeping Backyard Makeover contest. We've been trying to reach you." Kate remembered with a guilty pang the recent letter she'd dropped unopened in the trash, thinking it was an appeal to get her to subscribe to the magazine. It had never occurred to her that it might be about the contest.

"Congratulations!" Mr. Kessler went on. "I'm happy to inform you that you have won First Prize in the contest. A check for one hundred dollars will be in the mail to you shortly. You should receive it within ten days."

Kate was speechless. She had actually *won* something? "Thank you!" she stuttered. "Thank you so much!"

"You're very welcome. Oh, and another thing. We'd like to send a photographer to take a picture of you that we can use with an article about the contest for the June issue."

"I...I guess that would be okay."

"Great! I'll have him call you to set up a time. His name is Rick Tobey. Enjoy your new garden, Mrs. McIntyre."

Stunned, Kate sat there taking in the news. Who would have thought her little essay and hand-drawn sketch would come in first? Her vision of the newly created back yard was before her again. Only this time she could make it real.

She couldn't wait to tell Jerry and Earl and Mark. She looked at Nora, as usual banging her rattle on the front of the stroller. Robin had flung himself on the floor and was making siren noises as he steered his toy fire engine around the legs of the kitchen table. They'd be all right for the moment. She'd leave the door open to be sure.

She knocked on Jerry's door. "Jerry, are you there?"

When Jerry answered, Kate almost hugged her, but then thought better of it. They weren't really on hugging terms. "I've got the money for the back yard! I won a contest, do you believe it? The prize is a hundred dollars!"

Jerry looked bewildered, so Kate hastened to explain about the contest. "We'll be able to get lots of stuff now. Flowers, a picnic table, and what do you think about a white picket fence instead of chicken wire? Picture it, Jerry! A real backyard with a lawn and flowers and everything."

Jerry smiled at Kate's enthusiasm. "That sounds real nice, Kate."

"Oh, and we could probably get a sandbox, one of those with a cover so the cats roaming around don't pee in it." She glanced back through her own open door. The children were still engaged in banging and siren-ing.

"I have to get back before the kids realize I'm gone and start howling. We'll talk more about it later. And tell Earl, will you?"

Jerry nodded. She had the biggest smile on her face that Kate had seen yet.

Mark, too, broke into a surprised smile when she told him the news.

"I didn't tell you because I didn't really expect to win. But I didn't want to spoil my luck, just in case."

"That's great, Katie! I didn't know you knew about gardens."

"Well, I don't. Beginners luck, I guess." She shrugged. "So now we'll have the money for some decent fencing and flowers and all sorts of stuff. Maybe Earl can take Jerry and me shopping at Sears. Can you stay home with the kids some Saturday afternoon?"

Mark hesitated just for a moment. "Sure. I can get some typing done while they're napping. Just tell me when so I can let the study group know."

Study group…or Amanda?

She summoned up a smile. "I'll go see when Jerry and Earl can go. I hope as soon as the check comes."

A few days later, the check arrived in an official-looking brown envelope. Kate tore it open and her eyes went immediately to the amount. Sure enough, it was for $100. It was real.

The following Saturday Mark stayed home with the children while Earl drove Kate and Jerry to the Sears store in town. The seductive smell of hot buttered popcorn wafted over from the machine inside the door. Munching happily, each with a bag in hand, they wandered the crowded aisles in the garden center, picking out sections of white picket fence, a picnic table and umbrella, a plastic wading pool and pump, and a forsythia bush with its roots bundled up in burlap and tiny buds already showing on the branches. Sears was having a sale of lawn mowers, so they added the least expensive one to their booty.

As they were leaving, Kate heard someone call her name. She turned to see who it was. "Stu!" she said. "How are you? I haven't seen you for ages. How's the study group going? Mark says you're a good team."

"Hi Kate. Yeah, we get along pretty well." He hesitated. "Mostly, that is." He smiled at her sheepishly, peering at her through his thick horn-rimmed glasses. Mark had told her about Stu and the other guys being kind of nerdy, but they were all hard workers and smart, and he liked them a lot. So what did that 'mostly' mean? Something to do with Amanda?

But Stu was looking at his watch. "Sorry, Kate, I've got to go. Good to see you!" He hurried away down the aisle.

Kate looked after him, still speculating about what he'd meant.

Earl and Jerry had been inspecting the sandboxes.

"No sense spending a lot of money on one of them jerry-built excuses for a sandbox," Earl was saying. "I can make a better one than that, and a cover for it too, like y'all said you wanted. I'll pick up the lumber after work tomorrow."

He also said it was still too early for flowers. "My friend Jack said he'd give us some of his daisies and daylilies around Memorial Day weekend, and we can buy the annuals then too. Jerry here says she wants petunias."

Back home, they piled everything outside the fence line to wait until the grass had gotten a good start. "Probably a couple more weeks," Earl said. "But I can get going on the fence next weekend."

Kate and Jerry grinned at each other like co-conspirators. They'd done it! The garden was already taking shape before their eyes.

CHAPTER FIFTEEN

THE NEXT TUESDAY NIGHT, AFTER KATE GOT THE CHILDREN IN BED, LILY brought her schoolbooks over to study while Kate went to the Democratic Town Committee meeting. She was wearing a soft blue sweater, a favorite from college that she was careful to wear only when she went out without the children, safely out of range of baby drool and sticky little fingers. She had added a touch of lipstick and run a brush through her hair.

"Okay, I guess you'll do," she said to herself in the mirror.

As she walked down the street in the gathering dusk, she willed herself to ignore the ugly coal boxes and the tiny front yards of gravel and dirt. Instead, she lifted her gaze to the stars coming out above, and the streak of rose and lemon along the horizon, left by the setting sun.

It was dark by the time Kate picked her way across the field at the bottom of their street. But there was a hint of spring in the air, and at the thought of the garden, her heart lifted. Why the garden was so important to her, she didn't quite know. It must be in her genes, passed down from her farmer grandfather. She had a need to be outdoors, to see green things growing, to feel the sun on her face and to breathe this balmy spring air.

The smell of coffee greeted her when she pushed open the door at the Community Center. She felt a little nervous until she saw Barbara, who greeted her warmly and introduced her to two men standing nearby, whose names Kate promptly forgot.

"I'm on duty here at the door but save me a seat and I'll come join you when the meeting starts." Barbara nodded and smiled at two more people entering, and Kate found her way to a seat. There were about fifteen people seated in folding chairs, and a man fiddling with some papers at a table in front. Barbara joined Kate as promised when the man at the table called the meeting to order. She whispered that his name was Jim Macomber. He was tall, self-assured, with a blond crew cut and wearing glasses.

"As most of you know, we're in the process of recruiting people to run for several different offices in the coming election." The small room was warm from all the bodies, and he stopped to take off his sweater and toss it on a chair. He went on to name the potential candidates for the 12th District congressional seat, for the state legislature, for county sheriff, and, with a laugh, for dog-catcher.

"A lot of those Democratic slots have been vacant in recent elections, and it's time we got some Democratic names on the ballot. Let the Republicans know they're not getting a free ride."

There was enthusiastic clapping, then the meeting went on to address things like the cost of flyers, the current budget, and how many more block workers they would need.

"Speaking of which," he said, "please welcome Kate McIntyre, our newest block worker for Raleigh Court. Stand up, Kate, so we can all see what you look like."

Kate felt her face flush, but she stood and acknowledged the smiles around her.

Jim looked over at Barbara. "Kate was recruited by our indomitable vice chair!"

"Amazing the smart people you meet, doing laundry," Barbara said with a smile. "I was lucky to find Kate and have her actually willing to join this crowd. So treat her with respect, you guys!"

After the laughter died down, the discussion turned to national politics. Adlai Stevenson was still declining to run for president, though everyone there agreed he was the best possible candidate to lead the country in these dangerous times. American troops were still fighting in Korea, and the Soviets had claimed they had built an atomic bomb. Fears of a nuclear war had school children scrambling under their desks during air raid drills, and people building air raid shelters in their cellars.

Worst of all, Senator Joseph McCarthy was stirring up anti-communist hysteria by accusing people in the government, and actors, writers, and artists in Hollywood, of being left-wing traitors and spies. Kate had seen him on her friend Beth's new TV—the first set Kate had ever seen. Senator McCarthy's icy stare and venomous remarks had sent chills down her back.

They all thought that if only he would run, Stevenson was someone who could deal with Korea and the Soviet Union, put a stop to McCarthy's ravings, and bring people back to their senses.

After the meeting broke up, Kate stayed to chat with several people. She found them impressive: a law student, a couple of economics majors, a psych doctoral student, some political science majors like Barbara and Jim.

"Is everyone on the committee connected to the university in some way?" she asked Jim.

He nodded. "We haven't been able to interest any of the non-university people. It's hard to get to know them, much less get them involved in politics. There's this whole thing about the gulf between the auto workers who came north during the war, and the university students and their families. We'd like to register as many of the non-university folks as possible, get them to vote. Maybe they'd come to understand how important that is." He shrugged. "It ain't easy."

He stepped closer to Kate and looked down at her as if they were old friends.

"Maybe you and I could go call on some of them together sometime. I think we'd make a good team, don't you?" He grinned.

Kate had the uncomfortable feeling that he was flirting, but she wasn't sure. Instead of answering, she smiled and looked at her watch.

"Sorry, Jim. I have to get home to relieve the babysitter. See you next time."

On her walk home, she considered what had happened. Maybe she'd been wrong about Jim. Maybe he was just being friendly. She hoped so. It had been strange, and she had to admit, kind of nice, to have a man look at her as though she were an attractive woman. That hadn't happened in a while. Mark mostly took her for granted these days. Maybe she should wear the blue sweater and some make-up more often.

Despite the brief encounter with Jim, she felt energized by the meeting, mentally stimulated by the ideas tumbling in her head, in a way she hadn't since she left college.

At home, Lily was sitting at the kitchen table, hunched over her books.

"Everything all right?" Kate asked.

"Fine, ma'am. Kids didn't even stir. I checked on 'em a few times and they was—were—sound asleep." She started to gather up her books. "It's me that's having trouble." She shook her head, looking discouraged. "Can't seem to get this essay done."

"What's it about?" Kate extended her hand for the paper Lily handed her.

"It's supposed to be about your favorite place, and I wanted to write about Tennessee. But I couldn't figure out what to say."

"Why is it your favorite place?"

Lily shrugged. "I don't know. I guess because of the woods, and the little creek behind the house where I could go put my feet in the water when it was hot in summer, or go fishing with Pa." She stopped for a moment, and then her words came out in a rush.

"There's lots of birds there too, singin' like anything in the early morning. Once when I woke up real early, I went outside and saw a little baby deer at the edge of the woods, near the creek." A smile crept over her face. "I was only a little kid, but I remember it was like what you read in the Bible. The green pastures and still waters. Sorta like sacred." Her face flushed with embarrassment.

"Lily, that's beautiful! Just write it down the way you said it to me. You'll have your essay. You miss Tennessee, don't you?"

"Yes, ma'am. But it feels nice writin' about it." Her hazel eyes, so like Jerry's, got a dreamy look. "It's like I'm going for a visit back home." She slipped her sweater over her shoulders and flipped her hair free. It was red like Jerry's too, but deeper, more chestnut.

"I think I can do the essay now."

"Well, let me know if you'd like me to look it over after you're finished. And thanks for babysitting tonight. I was glad I got to go to the meeting. It was interesting."

Lily stopped at the door. "What was it about?"

"About the presidential election coming up next November, and about trying to get people to come out and vote."

"My teacher's been talking about that too. She says we should tell our parents how important it is."

"That's true. It's good you're discussing it in school."

Lily nodded. "By the way, my ma's been studying them—I mean those books you been loaning Danny. We were wondering if you got any different ones we could borrow."

"Of course!" said Kate. "You can borrow some any time."

Lily smiled. "My teacher likes to read poems to us sometimes. I like the sound of them."

"I have several poetry books, and some novels too. Come over some-time soon when it's not so late and we'll see which ones you'd like to borrow."

So, Jerry was teaching herself to read, just as Kate had suspected she might. With maybe a little help from Lily. She smiled with satisfaction at the thought.

After Lily had gone, Kate got undressed, dodging the damp diapers suspended from the line overhead. As she hung up her blazer and pleated skirt, some more relics from college days, she wondered if Jerry and Earl were registered to vote. That could be the starting point in her new role as a block worker.

Was she crazy to be taking on this volunteer job? Kids, husband, garden, endless housework, and never enough sleep. But better to plunge herself into some outside distractions than to sit at home brooding about Amanda.

CHAPTER SIXTEEN

MARK HAD JUST LEFT THE NEXT MORNING AND KATE HAD BARELY
swallowed her coffee when the phone rang.

"Hello, Kate. It's Peg." Mark's mother. Kate felt her stomach muscles
tighten. She pictured her mother-in-law: sharp-face, thin penciled
eyebrows, expertly rendered blond hair, the perpetual look of disapproval.

"I'm arriving day after tomorrow. I've already made a reservation at
the hotel in town. I'll be there at four in the afternoon."

Typical Peg. No 'How are you?' or any small talk. Right to the point.
And no asking whether this was a convenient time for Kate and Mark.

"That's fine, Peg. Are you driving?"

"Of course. How else?"

Well, there are trains and planes, Kate thought.

"I'm leaving first thing tomorrow and stopping over in Pittsburgh to
visit Doris."

Doris. Her childhood friend from when they both grew up in Millbury,
New Jersey.

Kate was surprised that they'd stayed friends for so long, even after
Doris had moved to Pittsburgh a few years ago. Maybe it was because they
only saw each other occasionally. As far as Kate could tell, Doris seemed
to be the only friend Peg had.

She hated to have to tell Mark that Peg was coming for one of her visits. There had always been a scratchy relationship between mother and son, with inevitable tension when they were together. But at least the visits were rare. Kate had spent only limited times with Peg since she married Mark but trying to withstand the constant put-downs was always a challenge. Nothing was ever right—Kate's clothes, her hair, her housekeeping, her parenting skills or lack thereof. Nothing was off limits where Peg was concerned.

Kate liked Mark's father, Robert. Always kind and affectionate to Kate, he was also about as henpecked a man as Kate had ever seen. Mark said his father had meekly agreed when Peg issued an ultimatum: they would not pay Mark's tuition if he majored in music, as he wanted to do. Only if he went to law school or medical school, or maybe engineering. Something that paid well. And had prestige, Kate had thought at the time. My son the doctor. Peg had been thrilled when the army sent Mark to pre-med and then medical school, and furious when he dropped out and enrolled at the university.

His two older brothers had not gone to college. There had been no money during the Depression to send them. Brian worked as a teller at their local bank in Millbury, and Paul was doing reasonably well as a contractor now that the war was over. Kate knew that neither job had the kind of status Peg had envisioned for Mark, and vicariously for herself. She saw herself as deserving a place in the small-town upper crust of society in Millbury and was only slightly mollified when he chose a business career instead. As he confessed to Kate, he'd watched his parents struggle during the Depression, when his father's small jewelry store almost went under, and Mark believed that unlike his father, with an MBA he could better navigate the financial world and make a good living.

When Kate broke the news that his mother was coming, Mark let out his breath in a long sigh. "Oh, God. No way to head her off, is there? She does that on purpose. Tells us at the last minute so we can't find an excuse for her not to come. How long is she staying?"

"I don't know. I was afraid to ask."

Mark put his arm around Kate. "I'm sorry I have to work Friday night and leave you alone to cope with her. It's lucky I can be here to share the pain on Saturday and Sunday."

Peg arrived Friday afternoon promptly at 4:00 o'clock as predicted. How could she do that? Kate wondered. Predict the exact time to the minute after driving for over four hours? She could even control time.

Peg came in briskly and gave Kate and Robin a brief hug. "Where's the baby?"

"She's napping, but she'll be awake soon," Kate said. "How was the trip?"

"The usual. Long and boring. I don't know why anyone lives in the Midwest. I checked into the hotel on my way in and made a reservation for dinner for all of us."

"Mark has to work, but the kids and I would love that." No cooking tonight. That was fine with Kate.

"Mark can surely take the night off to have dinner with his own mother," Peg huffed. "I assumed he'd already arranged it. He did know I was coming?" Her eyes drilled into Kate's as though to unearth some nefarious plot to foil her plans.

"Of course. But I don't know if he can take off from work. You can ask him. He'll be home in a little while."

In the children's room, Peg examined her granddaughter, whom she had only seen in pictures. "Still got that mop of black hair, does she? I thought it might have grown in more blond by now."

And where would that have come from? Kate wondered. Not from her or Mark, and not from Peg, whose blond hair came from a bottle.

She heard Mark letting himself in. "Kate? Mom?"

"In the kids' bedroom," Kate called.

Peg let Mark kiss her cheek. "How was your trip?" he asked.

"Why do people always ask that? It was the same as usual, as I told Kate. Long and boring," She turned to Kate. "Are you finished changing Robin yet? I don't know why that child is still in diapers. I had Mark trained by the time he was a year and a half." Poor Mark, thought Kate, not for the first time.

Mark sighed. "I'm sure you did. You even managed to control that."

"Now don't start with me, Mark. I'll not have any of your arguing the minute I get here."

"Okay, Mom. Truce." He gave her a half-hearted smile. "Sorry, but I have to go change for work and grab a bite to eat. We'll have more time to visit tomorrow. I'm not working this Saturday."

His mother raised her eyebrows. "I've made reservations for dinner tonight at the hotel and I expect you to join us."

"Can't do it, sorry. Can't afford to miss a night's pay, and anyway, I'd get fired if I took time off without notice." He disappeared into the bedroom.

"Stubborn as ever," Peg said.

Kate ignored the comment and headed to the kitchen to put Mark's dinner on the table. Only here an hour and already tension filled the air.

Dinner at the hotel was a treat for Kate and she was determined not to let Peg spoil it. She shut her ears when Peg complained to the waiter about the beef being overcooked, and when she demanded to know when Kate was going to start teaching Robin some table manners. Fortunately Robin was entranced with his Mac 'n' Cheese and chocolate milk and paid no attention. He was doing his best, spooning up his meal with only a few spills. Pretty good for a two-and-a half-year-old, in Kate's opinion. Nora sat tearing bread into tiny pieces and chasing peas around in the tray of her high-chair, which kept her occupied while the rest of them ate.

When Peg dropped them off after dinner, the quiet apartment was a welcome relief.

How many more days would they have to endure Peg's presence?

The next day, at Mark's suggestion, Peg drove them all to town, where Mark gave them a tour of the university campus, and Peg took them to lunch. A meal out in a restaurant, let alone two in a row, was so unusual that Kate determined to enjoy it no matter what. Mark did the same, and he and Peg kept their sparring to a minimum. Later, when they passed the School of Graduate Studies, Kate felt a stirring of the yearning that she'd experienced in her talks with Barbara Braden. She pictured herself back there in the classroom with Dr. Washburn, her favorite professor, surrounded by her fellow students, engulfed in passionate discussions and fierce arguments about whatever topic engaged them at the moment.

"I'd give anything to be able to go back to school," she made the mistake of saying.

"Well, that's hardly an option, is it?" Peg was quick to say. "You have two children and a husband to take care of, you know."

"I know," Kate said.

Mark reached over and patted her hand.

"You will, some day," he said softly. He knew how much Kate missed being part of the academic world.

Peg sniffed. "A woman's place is in the home, looking after her family."

Oh, right, barefoot and pregnant, Kate thought.

"So you'd better put the idea of going back to school out of your head, Kate."

Kate couldn't help it. "You want to bet?" she whispered.

But Peg, sitting in the back seat, didn't hear her. Which was probably for the best.

On Sunday, with Mark blessedly home again for the day, they took the children to the airport and sat in the viewing area, watching the giant planes take off and land. The Willow Run airport had been built early in the war, along with the adjacent bomber plant that had subsequently made headlines for a number of reasons, one of them being that at the height of production, the assembly line had produced B-24 bombers at the astounding rate of one every hour. Another claim to fame was its role in employing many women to replace the men who had gone to war. They became collectively known as Rosie the Riveter, and played a crucial part in filling manufacturing jobs, not only in Willow Run, but across the country.

As the great planes roared into the air, Robin was ecstatic, pointing to each one and shouting, "Airp'ane, big airp'ane, Daddy! Gamma, see the airp'ane?" His blue eyes were bright, and he looked so like his father, with his wavy brown hair and straight nose and slightly squared little chin, that even Peg softened enough to smile at his excitement.

Mark went back to school on Monday and Peg insisted on taking Kate and the children to the hairdresser in town. "Robin's hair needs a trim. And yours looks more like a sheep dog than a pixie cut," she observed tartly.

At least she didn't suggest getting Nora's little mop of fine dark hair styled. While the hairdressers worked on Kate and Robin, Peg picked up Nora and in a rare show of affection, cuddled her on her lap. And to her credit, she offered to pay for the haircuts. Her own bleached blond hair had been permed into submission, framing her face in tight curls. Her plump figure was firmly encased in a well-cut tweed suit. Kate looked down at her own dungarees and blue cardigan. No one would mistake her for a fashion plate.

Peg stayed for early dinner that night and a quick last visit with Mark before he went to work, then said her goodbyes. She was leaving on Tuesday morning, and Kate and Mark both breathed a sigh of relief. If they were lucky, life could return to normal for at least the next few months.

CHAPTER SEVENTEEN

BY THE MIDDLE OF THE FOLLOWING WEEK, KATE HAD HER PLAN IN PLACE. Sue would look after Robin and Nora for a day, and Kate would do the same for Sue's children the week after. On Thursday morning, while Mark swallowed his breakfast, she said she was taking the later bus to the university and could they meet for lunch.

Mark stopped with his spoonful of cereal in mid-air. "You're going to town?" he asked, surprised. "What for? You bringing the kids?"

"No, I have a couple of errands to do, and Sue offered to take Robin and Nora. So can we have lunch?"

"Sure." He had picked up his jacket and was heading for the door. "Drug store okay? What time?"

"Can you make it at noon? I should get the early afternoon bus back to Willow Run."

"Sure thing. See you later!" He gave her a quick hug and left.

Four hours later, Kate sat in a booth at the drug store in Ann Arbor, sipping a coke while she waited for Mark. He hurried in only a few minutes late.

"Sorry. I had to stay after class for a minute to see Professor Lehmann." He stooped to kiss the top of her head before sitting down across from her. "How did you make out with your errands?"

"I'll tell you after we order."

When their sandwiches came, Kate took one bite, and then drew a deep breath.

"I went to see Professor Washburn this morning. That's why I came to town. I made the appointment right after your mother left. Something she said about going back to school not being an option for me, started me thinking. Why isn't it an option?" She took Mark's hand in both of hers. Her words were coming faster now.

"Professor Washburn said he thinks I can get credit for the courses I already took. It's only been a little over three years since I dropped out. So I'd already have that many credits. It's too late to register for the fall term, but I could start next spring. He said I could audit his Constitutional Law course this fall if I want to, as sort of a refresher."

Mark was silent. Kate could see him trying to absorb what she had said. Finally he spoke.

"It's a lot to unload on me with no warning. Couldn't we have talked this over first?"

Just like when I called Sue about Jerry without asking Mark. "I'm sorry, but I wanted to find out first if it was even possible. That's why I asked if we could have lunch, so we could talk it over. I won't do it if you feel strongly that I shouldn't." Her heart sank as she said the words, but she wouldn't go against Mark in this. Maybe she'd have to wait her turn after he finished his degree.

"There are a lot of questions to be answered." Mark gave his head a little shake, as though to clear his thoughts. "What about the kids? And money? How would we pay for it? I think there are a lot of problems."

Kate let go of his hand and took another sip of coke. "Sue said she'd keep the kids on the days I have classes. By then Robin will be old enough to go to the coop nursery school at the Community Center along with Sue's older three. I could put in my volunteer day once a month when I don't have classes. I think that part would work. As for the money…" Kate took another deep breath. "I called my mother, and she and my father will loan me the money for tuition. I can pay them back when I'm able. My father said they owe me anyway, because I got scholarships and worked part-time so it didn't cost much to put me through the three years of school. Professor Washburn said he'd help me apply for a scholarship too. I think we could make it work."

This time Mark was silent for so long that Kate braced herself for what he was about to say. But finally he looked up and reached for her hand again and gave it a squeeze.

"If you're willing to take this on, besides all the other things you do, I'll help all I can. But we have a lot to work out first."

Kate jumped up and went around the table to hug him. "I know, and it won't be easy. But we can do it!" Kate had to stop and catch her breath. "There are a lot of possibilities. We just have to figure out what works for us."

They left the drugstore arm in arm, and as they stepped out on the sidewalk, a woman hurried past.

"Amanda?" Kate exclaimed.

Amanda turned around. "Mark? And Kate?" What are you doing in town?" She was looking at Kate.

"Having lunch with my husband," said Kate coolly. "How are you, Amanda?"

Amanda stared back her green eyes equally cool. "I'm fine. Gotta run." Her tone changed. "See you later, Mark." Her smile was directed solely at him.

Mark looked after her as she walked quickly away, an expression on his face that Kate couldn't interpret.

"What is it, Mark? What are you thinking?"

"Oh, nothing..." His voice trailed off. "It's complicated." He grasped Kate's arm. "Come on, there's your bus. We can talk more later."

But Kate wanted to say, later never seemed to come.

That night Kate waited up for Mark. As they were getting ready for bed, she asked him what he meant by the situation with Amanda being 'complicated.'

"Let's just say she's a troublemaker and leave it at that." He flopped down in bed and was asleep almost before the words were out of his mouth.

Troublemaker. What did that mean? Trouble for whom? Mark had sounded annoyed, but not at Kate. At least that was something. She remembered Stu's words when she bumped into him at Sears that time, about the study group "mostly" getting along. Again, she wondered if that had been about Amanda.

———

Kate had taken the plunge with her plan, and now she was ready to follow through. The following week she went back to the university and signed up to audit Professor Washburn's class in September. She imagined what it would be like, walking the children across the field and dropping them off at Sue's, then riding the University bus with Mark. Even though they would probably use the time on the bus to catch up on reading or studying for the next test, Kate loved that they would be doing it together. It helped erase the thought of Amanda still hovering in the back of her mind. With her new sense of resolve, Kate tried not to worry that the follow-up conversation about Amanda hadn't happened. It never seemed to be the right time. Mark left early every morning, came home for a quick dinner, then went to work. Usually by the time he came home after his shift, Kate was so tired she'd already fallen asleep. She had felt closer to Mark these past weeks, but she still didn't know what to think about him and Amanda.

Almost feverishly, she threw herself into the work in the garden and her volunteer work for the Town Committee. Barbara had asked her to get a list of registered Democrats from the county clerk so they could compare the names with residents of Willow Run Village. That way they could target those voters with reminders to vote and offers of rides to the polls and try to register as many of the other residents as possible. Earl offered to drive her to the county clerk's office on a day when he got home early. On the way, Kate asked if he and Jerry were registered.

"No, never bothered," he said. "Figured them politicians is all bums or crooks anyway."

"Well, some of them, but not all. You should get registered so you have some say about which ones get elected."

Earl wasn't interested, so Kate gave up for the moment. When she told Mark what Earl had said, he chuckled. "You have to admit he's got a point. Some of them *are* crooks or bums. Luckily Eisenhower isn't one of them, or Stevenson, if he can be persuaded to run."

CHAPTER EIGHTEEN

BY EARLY JUNE, THE GARDEN WAS COMING ALONG NICELY. THE PICKET fence was up, enclosing the delicate haze of green grass that had sprouted from the seeds they had planted in April. Earl had put in the forsythia, which valiantly produced a sprinkling of bright yellow blossoms, and helped Kate and Jerry position the picnic table near their back doors. He'd been working on the sandbox on weekends, and it was almost finished.

On an afternoon when both children were napping, Kate took the day's mail out to the garden and sat on the back steps while she opened the June issue of *Good Housekeeping*. Her own face, the picture Rick Tobey had taken weeks earlier, looked up at her from a corner of the cover. The caption read, 'Michigan Housewife Wins Garden Competition.'

Kate's throat constricted and she could hardly breathe. Her picture on a national magazine? It didn't seem real. She was still sitting there, staring in disbelief, when Jerry came out and sat down beside her. Wordlessly, her heart banging, Kate handed her the magazine.

Jerry's eyes widened in astonishment. "You're famous, Kate! Like those movie stars you see in magazines! Wait till Earl and Mark see this."

"I can't believe it." Kate shook her head. She looked at the cover again. "It says there's an article about it inside." She leafed through until she found the page. It was a short piece describing Kate's imagined garden and quoting some of her comments in the phone conversation with Brian Kessler. She was reading it aloud when the phone rang inside. It was her mother.

"Kate!" she said, without even saying hello. "I just got my *Good Housekeeping* and I couldn't believe my eyes when I saw you on the cover! What a surprise! I had no idea you'd entered. And such a nice article inside! I'm so proud of you, dear."

"Thanks, Mom. I never for a minute thought I'd win. And I had no idea they'd put my picture on the cover!"

"Well, congratulations. Your Grandpa would be so proud."

Mark and Earl were equally impressed when Kate showed them the magazine.

"Who knew I had a horticultural genius in the family?" Mark exclaimed. "My wife, who goes from collecting chicken poop to becoming a national celebrity!" He put his arms around her in a big hug.

Earl's response was that he knew what he was doing when he hooked up with a college girl as his gardening partner. "You got the brains and I got the brawn," he said with a chuckle. "Lucky thing we teamed up."

A few days later the mail brought several forwarded letters from *Good Housekeeping*, letters from readers who had read about Kate.

"I live in an apartment complex in the city," read one. "It's so ugly, with no grass or trees, and before I read the article about you, I just accepted that that was the way it was. Now I know I can do something about it, and I will!"

Another said, "I want to do what you did, but I don't know where or how to start. Can you advise me?"

Kate shook her head over that one. "I'm no expert, far from it," she said to Mark. "What do I tell this woman?"

"Just write and tell her step by step what you did and let her figure it out." He grinned. "Imagine, now you're getting fan letters!"

A few more letters arrived, and Kate answered all of them as best she could, happy to think that other women in various parts of the country were creating gardens of their own, not necessarily like hers, but just as important to them and just as soul-satisfying.

In late June, Adlai Stevenson was still declining to run, despite the urgings of President Truman and other party leaders. The Town Committee was circulating a petition in support of Stevenson, and Kate had been tapping on doors to ask people to sign. She had gone down one side of the street with discouraging results. Some of the university students and wives listened to what she had to say, then politely refused to sign. "No thanks, we're Republicans."

She even knocked on Annie's door, though she guessed it was probably futile, given their conversation months ago and Annie's superior attitude toward their Tennessee neighbors. She had guessed right.

"What made you think I would sign a petition for *him*?" Annie demanded. "John and I are voting for General Eisenhower, and you should too. He's a war hero, Kate! I'm surprised at you, going around knocking on doors for this other man. He shouldn't even be running against Ike. Everyone knows Ike's the best."

"It's a democracy, Annie. Remember? We get a choice."

As she walked away, Kate thought how far apart she and Annie were about things that really mattered. They had moved into Willow Run on the same day three years before and had met as they were lugging in suitcases and boxes of books and toys. Neither of them knew anyone in Willow Run, and they formed the habit of having coffee in the middle of the morning, several times a week. They helped each other figure out the mysteries of the wood and coal stoves, though Annie soon replaced both, and they borrowed back and forth, a cup of sugar or a stick of butter, when either of them ran out. Their conversations focused mainly on domestic topics— recipes for chili or spaghetti sauce, home decorating, or the latest fashions, which didn't interest Kate particularly. It was a relief to have an adult to talk to, but Kate had gradually realized, even before her disillusionment with Annie, that they didn't really have that much in common, or that many interesting things to talk about. Kate marveled now that they had ever been friends.

When she knocked on the next few doors, some people signed without hesitation, and Kate breathed a sigh of relief. But at other places, as soon as she mentioned "petition" or "Democratic nomination," the door got slammed in her face, sometimes with a curse or an annoyed "Not interested."

The following Saturday afternoon Kate set off to canvass the other side of the street. This time she took Robin with her while Nora napped, and Mark caught up on some studying. A woman opened one of the first doors she knocked on. Her stout figure was partially concealed by a clean gingham apron, and her hair had escaped in loose gray tendrils from a bun in back. The smell of something delicious wafted from the kitchen. The woman looked suspiciously at Kate's clipboard and started to close the door, but then she spied Robin.

"Afternoon, little fella. How old are ya?"

Clutching Kate's skirt, Robin smiled up at her.

"Say hello to the lady, Robin,"

He ducked his head shyly with a barely audible hello.

"He's two-and-a-half," said Kate, "and sometimes a little shy."

The woman clucked her tongue. "Well, but ain't you a big boy to go traipsing around with your Ma and that board she's carrying around. What you got there, anyway?" she asked Kate.

"I'm taking this petition around for people to sign. It's to try to get Governor Adlai Stevenson to run for the Democratic nomination for president."

"Never heard of him, but you seem like a nice girl so come on in and you can tell me about him." She looked down at Robin. "Would y'all like a piece of cornbread?"

Robin nodded. "Yes," he whispered.

"Well, come on then." To Kate she said, "S'cuse the mess. I just got done baking."

She ushered Kate and Robin into a sparsely furnished but neat apartment and sat them down at the kitchen table.

"I'm Kate McIntyre. I live down the street on the other side."

"My name's Ruby. Ruby Smith." She reached up and tucked the loose hair back into her bun. "Pleased to meet you. I think I've seen you go by a few times, pushing a stroller."

"Yes, I have a little girl, almost eight months old. Sorry we haven't met before."

"Yeah, well, I guess you're one of them college people. We don't have occasion to socialize much."

"I know, and I think that's too bad." Kate smiled up at Ruby as she set plates of fragrant cornbread on the table.

Robin began nibbling at his piece and Kate took a bite of hers. "This is delicious!" she said. Ruby's round face creased in a smile and she sat down beside Kate.

"So who is this man you're talking about?"

"His name is Adlai Stevenson. A lot of people think he would be a good president and they're hoping he'll agree to run in the November election. Are you and your husband registered to vote?"

"No ma'am. Some man come around and registered me and Bert in Tennessee, but we never got around to it here."

"Would you like to register? We have some people who can give you a ride to the town hall. That way, you'll be able to vote in November."

Ruby shook her head. "Don't know as I care about it. Lotta trouble and probably don't make no difference anyhow."

Kate tried to explain that if enough people vote, it *can* make a difference, but she could see she was getting nowhere until she mentioned that among other things, Adlai Stevenson supported more government help for the elderly.

Ruby perked up. "Well, that's somethin' me and Bert wouldn't mind havin.' Our son was laid off at the plant, and my husband Bert's been sick a lot. We're just gettin' by. Give me that thing and I'll sign it."

"But Ruby, I'm afraid you have to be a registered voter to sign the petition. Shall I have someone call and take you to the Town Hall?"

Ruby hesitated. "Well, yeah, I reckon. What did you say your name is?"

Kate repeated her name and wrote down Ruby's phone number, then thanked her for the cornbread. Robin swallowed his last bite and Ruby patted him on the head as they left.

Kate met with several more slammed doors, but also a few people who signed the petition. Two women, like Ruby, were initially suspicious, but charmed by Robin and his trusting smile, they were willing to listen to what Kate had to say. One of them was already registered and signed the petition. The other said she'd be willing to get registered, so Kate signed her up for a ride.

When they got home, they found Mark in the garden, chanting *"Ride a Cock Horse to Banbury Cross"* while he bounced a squealing Nora on his knee. Robin began hopping up and down and demanding his turn. "Okay, Buddy, you're next. But let me talk to Mommy for a minute first."

He set Nora down on the grass. "One big bonus of having a day off is that I get to do stuff like this. It's made me realize how much time I've missed with the kids."

"I know. But think how great it will be when you graduate next year and get a really good job and can be home every night and on weekends. And have time to play like this with Robin and Nora."

She looked across the garden, at Jerry's pink and purple petunias growing along her side of the fence.

"Wherever we end up, it will be hard to leave the garden. I'll just have to plant a new one at the next place we live. When I was out canvassing just now, I saw where someone had put two big pots of red geraniums on their front stoop. Maybe the garden idea is catching on."

She sat down on the steps. "It was quite an experience, seeing the reactions I got from knocking on peoples' doors."

Mark looked interested. "What happened?"

"Well, I got a few doors slammed in my face, and some angry responses. But I also got some more names on the petition, and two women who are willing to get registered. They both liked what I had to say about Stevenson. I just hope he can be persuaded to run."

Mark nodded. "I know you're a huge supporter, but I wonder how much chance he'd have of winning. He's such an intellectual. Witty and a great orator, but that might not win him votes with a lot of people. And besides, Eisenhower is such a popular figure."

Kate sighed. Mark was an Independent and liked to keep his options open. She didn't know if he'd vote for Stevenson or not. Still, he'd been supportive of her getting involved with the Democratic Committee.

"I know. But I think we have to try. Who else have we got?" She got up. "I'll go start supper. You can bring the kids in when I call." It was a welcome novelty, having Mark home for a leisurely dinner and not having him rush off to the plant afterward.

Someday, this would be their normal life.

CHAPTER NINETEEN

A FEW DAYS LATER, KATE HEADED DOWN THE STREET TOWARD THE grocery store, pulling both children in the wagon. As she was passing Ruby's, the door opened, and Ruby stuck her head out.

"How y'all today?" she called.

"Fine, Ruby. Isn't it great to see the sun?"

"Yes, ma'am, I sure get sick of Michigan winters. Where y'all off to?"

"The grocery store. You need anything?"

"No, thanks. Bert went yesterday after work. I'm bakin' some ginger-bread this morning. Come by on your way home and I'll have some for you."

Kate waved her thanks, and on her way home she stopped and knocked on Ruby's door. It opened immediately and Ruby handed her a basket of napkin-covered gingerbread. It smelled heavenly.

"My special recipe. Used to make it all the time in Tennessee." Her gaze was focused over Kate's shoulder, as though she was looking all the way to the Tennessee mountains.

"You know, Ruby, my next door neighbor is from Tennessee. Have you met her? Her name is Jerry Homan.

"No, can't say as I have."

"Well, you two should get together."

"Sure would like that. Why don't you bring her over tomorrow afternoon? I'll make us some sweet tea."

"Thanks, Ruby, I will. Wave bye-bye to Mrs. Smith, Robin."

Kate found Jerry on the back steps when she got home. Robin joined Danny in the sandbox and Kate sat down next to Jerry, with Nora on her lap.

"I just met a woman down the street who is from Tennessee. Her name is Ruby Smith. I told her you're from Tennessee too, and she wants us to come over tomorrow afternoon for sweet tea. Is that okay with you?"

For once, Jerry looked pleased instead of scared. "That would be real nice. How did you meet her?"

"I was knocking on doors, asking people if they want to register to vote, and if they'd sign a petition for Adlai Stevenson to run for president."

"Who's he?"

"Right now he's the governor of Illinois, but a lot of people think he should run for president. The only trouble is, so far, he says he doesn't want to. So we're gathering names on this petition to try to persuade him to run."

"So you think he's good?"

"I do." Kate repeated some of the things she'd said to Ruby and the other women.

Jerry was nodding her head in agreement.

"Jerry, you and Earl aren't registered, are you?"

Jerry shook her head.

"I asked Earl about it and he said he wasn't interested in voting. But you know, Jerry, it's important for all of us to use our vote to choose the next president. Otherwise we could end up with a dictator like Hitler."

"I'd be willing to do it, but Earl might get mad, so I better not."

"That's all right. But let me know if you change your mind. We have people who can drive folks to the Town Hall if they want to register." Kate stood up. "I have another Town Committee meeting tomorrow night. Do you think Lily can come over and stay with the kids again?"

"Sure, I'll tell her."

At Ruby's the following day, Jerry sat contentedly sipping sweet tea. She and Ruby had been sharing memories of Tennessee, the words pouring out as fast as their Tennessee drawl permitted. Kate smiled inwardly at how they had immediately connected.

"Whereabouts in Tennessee y'all from?" Ruby had asked.

"Auburnville," Jerry answered.

"Why, honey, that's almost right next door to Lynton Falls, where I'm from! We were practically neighbors!"

"I had a cousin who lived in Lynton Falls. I been there myself a few times." Jerry's eyes filled with tears.

Ruby had been about to refill their glasses, but now she leaned over and put her arms around Jerry. "Now don't you cry. Poor child, you're homesick, ain't you?"

Jerry choked out a yes, and then blew her nose and smiled. "It was just hearing the way you talk, like folks at home do, and then the names of those places. Kind of got to me for a minute. I'll be okay."

"Course you will. Now have some more tea and we'll see what else we both remember. What was your cousin's name? I knew just about every person in that little town."

Kate sat there listening to them reminisce, thinking how sad it was that these two women had lived on the same street for years and never met till now. So typical of the compartmented way we live in Willow Run. But now that they'd met, maybe they'd get together often. It sounded like they both needed a friend.

As though Jerry had read her mind, she stood up and said, "Miss Ruby, ma'am, I hope you'll come over to my place sometime soon and meet Earl and our girl Lily and our boy Danny. I'd be much obliged."

Ruby gathered her in another hug. "Don't you worry, honey, you bet I will."

"And bring Bert too, and your son. You said his name is Hank? Come Saturday when the men aren't working."

As they walked back up the street, Jerry said, "It meant a lot to me, meeting Ruby. Thank you, Kate."

"I'm so glad you two hit it off. I think she'll be a good friend to you."

That evening at the committee meeting, Jim Macomber complimented Kate on signing up seven people on Raleigh Court and getting a number of signatures on the petition.

"We were glad that some of those you talked to aren't connected to the university. As I told you, we've been trying to get some of our other neighbors involved, so this is a start."

He lifted his coffee cup in a salute. "Well done, Kate!"

Kate squirmed as the others turned to look at her. She wished he wouldn't single her out this way. Others on the committee had signed up people too.

The members of the committee went on to talk about having a fund raiser for flyers and other committee expenses. Maybe a picnic on the lawn outside the Community Center. They probably couldn't charge admission but could ask for donations. Someone suggested they might get Senator Blair Moody to come and speak. A former journalist, war correspondent, and Michigan senator, he was campaigning for a second term, and no doubt looking for votes. Jim said Moody was also currently working on his law degree at the university. He might be available, especially if the committee solicited donations for his campaign.

After the meeting, Barbara asked Kate what kind of reception she'd gotten when she canvassed her street.

"Some people slammed their doors, some politely said no, and some were very nice and listened to what I had to say. A mixed bag, I guess you'd say."

"Same reactions I got. But I think our efforts are paying off. At least we're calling attention to the election at a local level."

When Kate left, Jim followed her out. "Can I give you a lift?" he asked. "How about a cup of coffee on the way?"

They had just had coffee at the meeting, and where did he intend to find a place open for coffee at this hour? Certainly not on the way to her house, a few blocks away.

"No thanks. I can walk. It's only a short way." She started away at a brisk pace, but Jim fell in step beside her. "I'll keep you company then. Give us a chance to get better acquainted." He took hold of her arm.

Kate stopped walking. I don't want to get better acquainted, she thought. I just want to go home. And I don't want you holding on to my arm.

"Please, Jim…" she was starting to say, when to her relief, Barbara caught up with them. Kate pulled her arm free and began walking away.

"Good night, you two," she said over her shoulder. "See you at the next meeting."

She felt embarrassed by Jim's attention and what she was sure now was flirting. He was attractive, no denying it, but she was not interested. She hoped she had discouraged him enough so that it wouldn't happen again, and they could continue to work together on the Committee.

In a flash of enlightenment, she realized that maybe it had been like that for Mark and Amanda. Maybe Mark had been walking this tightrope between keeping Amanda as a working partner and fending off her advances. Ironic, if true, that it should have happened to both her and Mark.

When she got home, Lily said she'd just checked, and the kids were fine. She'd finished her homework and was reading *Little House on the Prairie* by Laura Ingalls Wilder, one of the books Kate had loaned her.

"I like reading about the time when people were moving West and were afraid of Indians, but kept going anyway, and how the neighbors helped when the family got sick and stuff. It used to be like that in Tennessee."

"I loved that book too." Kate picked it up and gazed at the cover. "I couldn't bear to get rid of it, so that's why I still have it. I'm keeping it for Robin and Nora. You're probably a little old for it, but I think it's a book anyone can enjoy."

She reached for a package wrapped in blue tissue paper and tied with blue yarn that was on the kitchen shelf. "I got you something for your birthday. Your mother said it's tomorrow. Thirteen, right? Happy birthday, Lily!"

Lily tore off the paper and took one look at the cover, then hugged it to her. "*Anne of Green Gables*! My teacher told me about it, and I been wanting to read it. I was going to get it from the library, but now I have my own. This is the best birthday present ever. Thank you, Kate!"

Kate had felt a little guilty spending some of their dwindling cash on the book, but Lily had been baby-sitting for her on several Tuesday nights, and other times as well, and Jerry refused to let her take any money. "She don't do nothing, just sits there and reads, same as she would at home."

With Lily's love of books, Kate felt this was the least she could do.

CHAPTER TWENTY

BY EARLY AUGUST, THE DEMOCRATIC COMMITTEE'S ACTIVITIES HAD picked up. Adlai Stevenson, in spite of his reluctance, had been drafted at the Democratic National Convention in late July to run for president. The convention was held in Illinois, and as governor, Stevenson gave the welcoming address, a speech so powerful and stirring that it unleashed a flood of demands that he become the candidate. After a final conversation with President Truman, who again urged him to run, Stevenson accepted the nomination.

The Democratic Committee was asking for volunteers to help put up campaign posters and to distribute flyers. After one of the meetings, Barbara asked Kate, "What's going on with you and Jim? You seem to be high on his list of favorites."

"Nothing's going on. I wish he'd stop flirting, or whatever it is he thinks he's doing. I've tried to let him know in a nice way that I'm not interested, but he doesn't seem to get the message."

"Maybe because you're so darned cute." Barbara grinned. "He's really a nice guy, just a little dense sometimes. He'll get it eventually."

The next time Jim offered to walk Kate home after a meeting, she stopped and looked up at him.

"Thanks anyway. It's just a short way and I'll be fine. Good night." She hoped he'd gotten the message.

A few days later, Kate took Nora and Robin and started down the street to distribute new flyers supporting Stevenson. She had stopped at one or two houses when Jim pulled up beside her in his car.

"Want some help?"

"No, thanks, I can manage."

"Well, four hands are better than two and it will make the work go faster."

He got out of the car. "Come on, Kate, I don't have to be at the university for another two hours, and I just want to help."

It was close to lunchtime and the kids would be hungry and cranky if she didn't get them home soon. She really could use the help.

"Okay, then. If you could take the other side of the street, I'll do this one."

They made their way down opposite sides of the street and when Jim reached Ruby's house, she opened the door. She was frowning.

"Whatever you got there, young man, I don't need it." She started to close the door.

"Ruby, Jim's a friend of mine," Kate called. "We're passing out flyers about the election." She pushed the stroller across the street, with Robin tagging along, and introduced Jim and Ruby to each other.

"I'm pleased to meet you, ma'am." Jim smiled at Ruby. "Kate's told me about you. We have you on the list for a ride to get registered."

"Yeah, Kate talked me into it. She's a nice girl, so I said I'd go along with it."

"I'm glad you did. We need all the help we can get with this election." He shook Ruby's hand. "See you at the polls!"

When all the flyers had been distributed, Kate and Jim walked back to his car.

"Cute kids," Jim said as he got in. "You're lucky."

"Do you have children?"

"No, divorced. I live in the men's dorm here, but I'm moving to an apartment in town with a friend."

"What about the committee?" Jim's place would be hard to fill.

116

"Oh, I won't move till after the election."

"Good. We need you."

She was relieved that this time no flirtatious hints were coming her way.

Late in the afternoon Kate went out to the garden. Jerry was already sitting on the step and moved over to make room for her. Kate sat down, the concrete pleasantly cool on her bare legs. She closed her eyes gratefully, breathing in the fragrance of grass and flowers. Jerry seemed to read her thoughts.

"You did a grand thing, making this garden," she said. "This is the first time I've enjoyed summer since we moved from Tennessee."

"Me too. We need grass and flowers to make up for these cold Michigan winters."

"There's another thing I want to thank you for." Jerry gave Kate a shy smile. "We never spoke about it, but you prob'ly guessed that I couldn't read. I never had much schooling to speak of, but I been studying the books you loaned Danny and Lily, and Lily's helped me some, so now I can pretty much make out the words and understand the stories. Even the words to the hymns. I can figure them out now. If it wasn't for you, I'd never've learned to read."

"I'm so glad the books helped. Which one did you like best?"

"*Anne of Green Gables*, I guess. Me and Lily have been reading it out loud together. Anne reminds me of Lily sometimes, kinda feisty. And the woman who adopts her, Marilla, is sort of crusty but good-hearted underneath, like some of the women I knew in Tennessee."

"I have another book I think you'd like. It's called *To Kill a Mockingbird* and it takes place in the South." She got up. "I'll bring it over later. It's about a little girl whose father is a lawyer who defends a black man accused of murder. We can talk about it after you read it, if you like." She went back inside, wondering what Jerry's reaction would be to this story of racial discrimination.

117

CHAPTER TWENTY-ONE

THAT EVENING AFTER DINNER THE PHONE RANG, AND WHEN KATE answered, a familiar voice said in strident tones, "I need to speak to Mark."

"Mark's not here, Peg. He's at work."

"Where can I reach him? I have to talk to him."

Did she think Mark had a phone sitting conveniently next to him on the assembly line?

"He's not near a phone. Is something wrong?"

"You can say that again." Her voice rose. "Robert has taken leave of his senses. He walked out on me and went to stay at Vicky's."

Vicky. Mark's father's assistant at the jewelry store, a mousy woman of indeterminate age who had worked for him for decades. Kate struggled to imagine such an unlikely event. Robert at Vicky's? She groped for words.

"I'm sorry, Peg. I'm sure you must be upset. Is there anything I can do? Have you called Brian or Paul?"

"Don't be an idiot. They're useless. Tell Mark to call me when he gets home. No matter how late." She banged down the receiver.

Kate was stunned. Timid, meek Robert. Where had he found the courage to walk out on Peg? Not that she blamed him. Far from it. Peg had been driving him to it for years.

Kate left a note for Mark to phone his mother, no matter how late. "Wake me when you get home. I'm going to try to get some sleep."

Sometime during the night, Kate half woke and heard the mumble of Mark's voice in the living room, but she fell back to sleep and he didn't wake her. She was in the kitchen next morning, starting the coffee, when he stumbled out of the bedroom.

"Mom says Dad left while she was out at her bridge club. He took some clothes and a few books and nothing else. She wants me to come to New Jersey and talk him into going back home." He yawned and rubbed his eyes. "God, do I need that coffee."

He poured himself a bowl of cereal. "I told her I can't possibly go, and to talk to Brian and Paul, which of course she refuses to do." He gulped the rest of his coffee. "I can't believe Dad had the nerve to leave. I never once heard him oppose anything Mom did or said. Not once." He smiled briefly. "I feel like telling him, 'Good for you, Dad. Don't let her bully you!'"

Kate knew what a struggle Mark's childhood had been. He had grown up watching his father and his two older brothers dominated by their mother, the subjects of her constant tirades about their many failings and her insistence on controlling every aspect of their lives. Mark had vowed he wouldn't let her do that to him. It had led to some angry confrontations when Peg listened in on his phone calls, criticized the friends he chose, or the way he wore his hair and his too-casual clothes. Mark reacted by spending more and more time at the library, or hitting balls on the tennis court, or staying with friends. When he was home, he learned to turn a deaf ear to Peg and refused to respond to her verbal attacks. The Army had been his ultimate escape.

Now, Mark stood up. "Gotta go. If she calls again, tell her I'll call when I get home from school."

Later, out in the garden, Kate let Robin help her pull the last of the summer's weeds from the flower bed. Earl's friend had been as good as his word and given them daisies and daylilies that had lighted up the garden all summer with bright patches of yellow and orange and white. Down on her hands and knees, Kate showed Robin which plants were weeds, and together they yanked them out. As she dug her fingers into the warm soil

120

and inhaled the rich scent of earth, biblical words, slightly altered, floated into her mind: It restoreth my soul.

Robert called before Mark got home. His voice was as calm and serene as ever. "I just wanted to let you know that I've moved out and I'm staying temporarily at Vicky's."

"Yes, we know, Dad. Peg called last night. Mark's not home from school yet. Are you all right?"

"Better than I have been in a long time. Please have Mark call me when he gets home."

When Mark talked to him later, Robert said he was sorry, but he couldn't stay with Peg any longer. She had decided to turn his workshop in the basement, where he sometimes worked on his jewelry, into a recreation room and bar, a place where she could entertain her society friends. Not that she had any, Robert had added.

It was the last straw, he told Mark. Peg hadn't even discussed it with him, just had an architect and decorator show up and start making plans. After she left for her bridge game, Robert had packed his suitcase and gone to Vicky's. She'd kindly offered him a place to stay till he figured out what to do.

"So what are you going to do now?" Mark asked.

"I don't know. I have to think about it. I'll be in touch, son."

Mark had hardly hung up when Peg called. He beckoned to Kate to come close so she could hear too. Scorching words came spewing out of the phone as Peg launched a diatribe against Robert, against Brian and Paul, and finally against Mark.

"All you care about is that go-nowhere job, and your classes at school. You care nothing about me and what I'm going through. Well, I'm not staying here to let all the old biddies gossip about me. I'm getting out before they have a chance to stick up their noses and snub me." She stopped for breath. "Get the bedroom ready for me. I'm leaving tomorrow and driving straight through."

"You can't do that, Mom. It would be much too crowded." By now he was shouting. "We can't have you here. It's not an option."

But Peg had already slammed down the receiver.

Mark and Kate looked at each other, momentarily speechless.

"What are we going to do? How can we stop her? If she moves in, we'll end up killing her, or each other." He put his head in his hands. "Ah, shit."

"I do know one thing," said Kate. "If she does come, I'm leaving." She thought for a minute. "What about her friend Doris? Maybe your mother would go stay with her in Pittsburgh for a while. We could call Doris and ask."

Mark sat up. "It's worth a try. We could offer to share expenses." He was looking a little more cheerful.

"Good idea. But where would we get the money?"

Mark's face broke into a feeble grin. "Ask my dad? A double bonus. He can help pay Mom's expenses and not have to worry about her trying to drag him back home. And we won't have her living here with us."

He picked up the phone. "Do we have Doris's number?"

Kate found it for him. "Hello, Doris?" he began. "It's Mark, Peg's son. Yes, it has been a while." He rolled his eyes at Kate. She could hear Doris going on and on about her son in Idaho and her daughter in Texas, until Mark was finally able to break in.

"I'm calling about Mom. No, she's all right. It's just that she and my dad have split up…yes, separated, and she needs a place to stay for a while. We thought maybe she could come visit you. It might cheer her up."

Doris was slightly hard of hearing and her voice carried all the way across the room.

"I guess it would be all right. I have my guest room where she usually stays, and it would be nice to have a longer visit."

"Do you think you could call her tonight? It might come better from you than from me." He hesitated a second. "You don't have to tell Mom I called you. Say you heard it from someone in Millbury."

"All right, Mark. I'll do that." She started to hang up, then said, "Why did they split up? I talked to Peg a few days ago and she didn't say anything."

"We don't know yet. Mom can tell you all about it when she comes. Thanks, Doris! You've just done your good deed for the year."

Mark hung up with a sigh of relief. "Katie, you're a genius. What made you think of Doris right away?"

"I guess because she's the only real friend Peg has, so she was our only chance."

They didn't hear from Peg for the next few days. Brian said the house was locked and Peg's car was gone, so he assumed she'd decided to drive herself to Pittsburgh. When Mark got in touch with Doris, she said Peg was there but didn't want to talk to anyone.

Later that week, Robert called again. "I've made some big decisions. I'm going to sell the store and use the money to buy a camper. I've been thinking of retiring anyway, and I'd like to do some traveling while I'm still healthy enough to enjoy it. Maybe I'll go to Florida. Play some golf. Soak up some sun. Look up some of my friends from Millbury that have retired down there." He cleared his throat. "I'm sorry about your mother. It's just as well she left town for a while. I'm sure it was the gossip that worried her the most."

"That's great, Dad! Good for you. Will you have enough to live on and still keep up with Mom's support?"

"Yes, with the money from the store and my pension, I'll be fine."

"Well, put us on your itinerary when you start traveling. You can park the camper right at our curb and have a good visit with your grandchildren."

He hung up and said to Kate, "I can't believe he had the guts to stand up to Mom." He shook his head. "Amazing!"

And the meek shall inherit the earth, Kate thought, or at least find a way to out-maneuver the formidable Peg.

CHAPTER TWENTY-TWO

LATER THAT WEEK, KATE AND THE CHILDREN LEFT FOR THEIR ANNUAL two-week visit with her parents in Connecticut. Her mother had sent train tickets for the three of them. Mark remained in Willow Run; he couldn't afford to miss work or his summer classes.

"I'll be fine," he'd said to Kate, "and don't worry, Earl and I will take good care of the garden."

And would Amanda be taking good care of Mark? But Kate refused to let the thought spoil the trip.

Robin could hardly contain his excitement as they waited on the platform for the train to New York, where Kate's father would meet them.

"Here it comes, Mommy! I see the big engine!" As the train thundered in, whistle wailing, he backed up against Kate and covered his ears, his eyes wide.

The train came to a stop amid swirling puffs of steam, and Mark lifted Robin aboard and helped Kate get herself and the children settled.

"Bye, Robin, have fun with Grandma and Grandpa." Mark kissed all of them goodbye and jumped off the train as it began to move.

Robin waved from the window until Mark was a just dot in the distance, then turned his attention to their compartment. He was fascinated by the way the seats pulled down to make beds, and by the tiny lavatory and washbasin in one corner.

Dinner in the dining car was another adventure, especially the finger bowls with their floating slices of lemon. Robin lifted his bowl and started to drink.

"No, honey, these are finger bowls for rinsing your fingers if they get sticky from food," Kate explained. Intrigued, Robin dipped his forefinger in and licked off the lemony water.

At bedtime, the porter made up their beds. Robin and Nora soon fell asleep, lulled by the rhythm of the wheels, but Kate dozed fitfully through the night as the train bumped over crossings, and passed through unknown towns with darkened streets and stations where lights washed through the compartment and were gone.

Her father was waiting at the station in New York. The lines in his face had become a little deeper, but he was wearing the familiar University of Michigan sweatshirt that Kate and Mark had sent him, and his well-worn Yankees baseball cap was clapped on over his bald spot. A neat salt-and-pepper fringe of hair showed beneath it.

Kate rushed into his arms, with a protesting Nora crushed between them.

"Hey, Nora, don't cry. I'm your grandpa and you are about to take a ride in my Jeep! Would you like that?" He grinned down at Nora and tweaked her nose.

Nora looked up, uncomprehending, but allowed him to lift her onto Kate's lap when they reached the car.

"And you, young man, will sit right behind me and make sure I go the right way."

"Okay." Robin climbed into the back seat and sat up straight and tall, trying to look important.

As they drove away from the station, through the traffic, and swooped across the state line into Connecticut, Kate looked out the window at the remembered landscape, increasingly small town and rural along the coastline. Her parents' house, where she had grown up, had been built back in the 1920s. White, with green shutters, it hadn't changed much. The portico over the front door divided the house in two, with identical sets of windows staring out through the trees like eight pairs of eyes. The branches of a sycamore tree still brushed against the window of her childhood bedroom, and she remembered lying in bed with her head on the windowsill on hot summer nights, looking up through the leaves at the moon and a sky full of stars. She felt a stab of nostalgia for those untroubled days.

When they entered the house, the aroma of coffee wafted from the kitchen. Kate's mother hugged Robin and kissed Nora before taking Kate in a tight embrace.

"I'm so happy you're here!" she said, her eyes a little misty. They hadn't seen each other since the previous October when her mother had taken a week off from her library job to help Kate when Nora was born. Over the years, her mother's short hair had grayed, like her father's, and was combed back in silver waves from a still youthful face. Kate always loved her mother's smile, which revealed a dimple in her cheek and made her look slightly mischievous.

"I know. I'm happy to be here too, Mom. And thanks for the train tickets. Robin was so excited about going on a train." She gave her mother another hug. "I smell coffee, and are those your cinnamon pecan buns I see on the table?"

The next two weeks were a series of sunny days at the beach, where Robin dug in the sand and made sandcastles, and Nora plopped down at the edge of the water, babbling delightedly as the shallow waves washed over her feet.

One day they packed a lunch and went out on Kate's father's boat. They anchored beside a small island and went ashore to swim from the beach, with Robin squealing happily as he paddled about in his plastic tube. Another time they built a fire on the beach, the way Kate remembered from her own childhood, and toasted marshmallows for S'mores.

It was a blissful change for Kate, away from the rigors of life in Willow Run. Her mother insisted on taking care of grocery shopping and meals, and her father had done the dinner dishes as long as Kate could remember.

"You can clear the table and scrape the dishes," he told Kate. "And then get out of my way!"

He said he liked doing dishes, standing there with his hands in hot soapy water and his mind free to wander wherever he wished it to go.

They paid a visit to Kate's grandmother, who still lived in the colonial farmhouse a few miles away where Kate's mother had grown up. The family had started calling her GeeGee when she became a Great-Grand-mother. She was an energetic little woman with a thick head of white hair that had once been dark like Kate's. People said they resembled each other, which Kate took as a great compliment.

GeeGee set out milk and a molasses cookie for Robin, then the two of them went off to pick the wild beach plums growing on the nearby sand dunes. Kate and her mother poured glasses of iced tea and sank into lawn chairs under the big maple tree by the house.

"How's everything with you these days, Kate? We haven't had much alone time to just talk. How's Mark?"

Kate hesitated. "OK, I guess." She paused. "It's been hard, with Mark at the university all day and the auto plant at night. We don't have much time for just the two of us. Even on weekends, he goes to the university library, sometimes to meet with his study group. It's difficult to even find time to have a conversation." Again, she hesitated. "The study group includes a sexy-looking blond named Amanda who seems very interested in Mark. She's even flirted with him right in front of me." She shook her head. "Makes me want to smack her and tell her to back off, he's not available."

Her mother considered what she had said. Then, like Sue, she asked, "What does Mark say?"

"He's kind of evasive and says not to worry, she's not his type, and then he changes the subject or goes off to bed." Kate sighed. "I don't know. I'm not sure what to think."

Her mother was silent for a minute, then she reached over and put her hand on Kate's knee.

"This reminds me of something that happened years ago to me and your dad, when you were about seven or eight years old. It had to do with one of the teachers in your father's school."

Kate sat up straight. "One of Dad's teachers? I know they all adored him. I remember you told me how several of them gave him their food coupons during the war so he could have all those cups of coffee every day."

"Yes, but there was one who apparently thought she was someone special. I'd see her sometimes at the potluck dinners or faculty parties, finding ways to sit next to him, or putting her hand on his arm and leaning towards him as though they had secrets to share. She was quite attractive and very well-endowed."

She frowned slightly, remembering. "When I asked your father about it, he just laughed and turned it into a joke. 'Oh, that's just Millie being Millie. She'll get over it one of these days.'"

"But I wasn't so sure. She didn't seem to be 'getting over it,' and instead it kept getting worse. She started calling Dad at home and making up excuses to talk to him. I finally had enough, and I confronted him.

"'I don't know if anything is going on between you and Millie,'" I said, "'but I need you to tell me one way or the other.

"It turned out that your dad had no interest in Millie and had been trying to gently fend her off without creating a scandal. But he said she'd begun coming to his office after school hours when he was working late, suggesting they go out for coffee, or asking his advice about this and that. He said he finally had to do something about it."

Kate was sitting immobile with shock at the revelation of this hitherto unknown side of her father. "I remember sensing something was wrong for a while back then," she said. "But it was just a vague feeling, awkward pauses at the dinner table, or you and Dad not saying much to each other. But then it passed, and I forgot about it. So what happened?"

"Dad asked the Superintendent to transfer Millie to another school and that was the end of it. Dad said he hadn't told me about it because it was so uncomfortable and embarrassing, and he thought the less said about it the better. But the talk we had really cleared the air, and things were okay after that."

She took a deep breath. "I think you need to do the same with Mark. Make a time to face him with your worries, get it out in the open and let him know how you feel."

Kate sat thinking about what her mother had said. "You're right, Mom. I *have* tried to do that a couple of times, but mostly I've been tiptoeing around the subject of Mark and Amanda, worrying because I've been afraid of what I'd find out. And then what was I going to do?" She gazed up through the green canopy above her. "I shouldn't have waited so long."

She picked up their empty glasses and stood up. "Thanks, Mom." She leaned over and kissed her mother's cheek. "It helped to hear about you and Dad."

GeeGee and Robin appeared just then, carrying pails brimful of beach plums.

"GeeGee and I are going to make beach plum jelly," Robin told Kate, a smile spreading across his face, "and I'm going to put some on my toast at breakfast!"

On their last day, Kate and her mother sat at the kitchen table, having a last cup of coffee and talking about plans for Kate's visit the following summer.

"Maybe we can make it a family reunion," Kate suggested. "We'll get JoAnne to come from Texas and Larry and his family from California. They haven't seen Robin since he was a baby, and they've never even met Nora. And by then I hope Mark can come too. We might even fly!"

It would be something to look forward to during the endless Michigan winter.

The next morning, Kate's mother stood on the front steps, waving them off. As the car pulled away, she called after Kate, "Don't forget to have that talk!"

The return trip to Michigan seemed long and tiring, and with the novelty worn off, Robin was cranky and complaining. It was a welcome relief the next morning to see Mark sitting on a bench on the station platform, looking eagerly at the train windows to try to spot them. When he got up and walked toward the train, Kate was struck by the easy grace with which he moved through the world, comfortable, in spite of his limp, in his athlete's body, honed by years of tennis in high school and college.

When they descended from the train, he scooped up Robin, then enveloped all three of them in a bear hug.

"Welcome home," he whispered in Kate's ear. "I've missed you."

She closed her eyes and rubbed her cheek against the soft fabric of his shirt, breathing in the familiar Mark scent of shaving lotion and soap and a faint aura of coffee.

Mark smiled down at her. "I borrowed Stu's car to come meet you. So let's go home and you can check out whether Earl and I did a good job with the garden."

Indeed they had. The grass was freshly cut, the flowers bright and welcoming. Kate sat down in one of the lawn chairs and sighed gratefully. It was good to be home.

Curled up in bed with Mark that night, Kate let her anxiety about Amanda go, at least for now. The talk with her mother, and the two weeks away from Mark, had given her a new perspective. She hadn't wanted to spoil this homecoming, but she made a vow to herself that she would have that conversation with Mark at the first opportunity.

She was smiling when she fell asleep.

CHAPTER TWENTY-THREE

Two days later, Kate sat on the back steps, waiting for Mark to come home. He'd said he'd be taking the early bus, so Kate had decided that today was the day to talk about Amanda and finally get at the truth.

Earl had mowed that morning, and the pungent smell of fresh-cut grass lingered on the air. Robin and Danny were playing in the sandbox, and Nora was sitting on a blanket on the grass, crowing happily, with multiple toys and stuffed animals within reach. She'd been crawling for a while now, but at ten months had not yet started to pull herself up on the furniture, as Robin had done.

Soaking in the rays of the late summer sun, Kate knew she should be feeling relaxed and content. But two things had happened that morning. First, she and Mark had had a rare argument over something so trivial Kate didn't even remember how it started. Something about laundry, that was it. Mark didn't have any clean underwear. Kate had hauled the laundry over to the Laundromat the day before, but it had been rainy and muggy, and the clothes hadn't dried.

"So what am I supposed to wear?" Mark had shouted. And Kate had yelled back, "How do I know? Wear them wet! They'll dry."

Mark had slammed the screen door when he left, without saying good-bye. Kate wondered if he'd chosen to wear the wet underwear or the ones from the day before, but she really didn't care. It was ridiculous that they'd argued over something as silly as underwear. They'd probably laugh about it later.

Also that morning, Kate had seen something that raised new questions about Amanda. She had arranged before her trip to Connecticut to leave the children at Sue's and without telling Mark, take the later morning bus to town. His birthday was the next day, and when she'd been Christmas shopping last December with Sue, she'd seen a handsome briefcase in the window of a leather goods store. Of soft brown cowhide, burnished to a beautiful shine, it was the perfect gift to replace the battered knapsack that Mark had been carrying all through college: Kate had saved for the brief-case for months, a dollar here and a dollar there, mostly squeezed from the grocery money.

When she reached the shop, to her relief the briefcase was still in stock. Kate spread out her pile of bills and paid for it, then with a satisfying feeling of Mission Accomplished she headed for the bus stop, carrying the briefcase in a large shopping bag,

As she was boarding the bus, she stopped short. Mark and Amanda were standing on the street corner a block away, deep in conversation. Or an argument? She couldn't see Mark's face, but she could tell by the stiff way he was holding himself that he was angry. Amanda was waving her arms in the air and shaking her head furiously.

At that moment, the bus door closed behind Kate, blocking her view. She sat down by a window and as the bus took off, she wondered what on earth Mark and Amanda were saying, and what was making Amanda so angry. A vague shadow of her old anxiety hovered in the air. She would know soon enough, when Mark came home, if it was justified.

Now, as she waited in the garden, the time for the 5 o'clock university bus came and went and no Mark. Where could he be? Maybe the bus was late. She took Nora and a protesting Robin back inside to be near the phone in case Mark called. As the minutes turned into a half hour, then forty-five minutes, panic set in. Her imagination went wild. Could he have gone off somewhere with Amanda? Judging by the scene she'd witnessed earlier, she thought that was not much of a threat anymore. Maybe he was still so mad from this morning that he wasn't coming home. But that didn't seem likely either. It had been such a stupid argument.

If only she knew somewhere or someone to call to find out if he'd been on the bus. She wracked her brain, trying to remember someone they knew who rode the same bus with Mark. Bill Somebody. What was his last name? She couldn't think.

It was almost six o'clock when the phone rang. Kate had been pacing to and fro, trying to stay calm and not frighten Robin. She jumped when the sound pierced the air and then snatched up the receiver.

"Kate? It's Hal. I'm at the hospital. Stay calm, but there's been an accident. The bus from the university ran off the road, and they brought some of the injured here. I'm afraid Mark's been hurt. It looks like some sort of head injury, maybe a hematoma—bleeding in the brain. We're waiting for the results of the x-rays...Kate, are you there?"

"Yes, I'm here." Her voice was faint. She could hardly talk over the pounding of her heart. "How bad is it? Is he conscious?"

"No. He was lucid when he first came in, but he's lapsed into a coma. He could come out of it any time. We just don't know yet how bad it is. I ordered the x-rays, and have a neurosurgeon coming to see him, but Kate —try not to worry. Save it till we know for sure what's going on."

Kate drew in a shaky breath. "I'll try."

"And listen, Sue is on her way over to your place. She's coming with you to the hospital. I had her call a cab."

The taxi drew up just as Kate hung up. Sue came in and hugged Kate hard. Her brown eyes were compassionate. "Hal says it could be a lot worse," she said. "Mark may even be conscious by the time we get there."

Kate looked at her blankly, barely able to understand what Sue was saying.

"Oh, and I called Jerry. She and Lily will be over in a minute to stay with the kids.

Kate felt too dazed to think. Her hands had turned to ice and her feet felt too heavy to lift. She heard Jerry and Lily come in from next door, and Sue giving instructions about Robin and Nora, but she couldn't seem to focus on anything but Mark. *Mark, don't leave me, she prayed. Please be all right.*

"I'll call you from the hospital," Sue told Jerry. She took Kate's arm and steered her toward the door.

"No!" Kate cried. "Wait…" she rushed back to where the children sat playing on the living room floor and gave each of them a kiss. "Mommy will be back soon," she said, over the sob rising in her throat.

When they got to the hospital, Hal said Kate could take a peek at Mark, but a nurse was monitoring him, and they were expecting the neurosurgeon any time. Kate would have to wait in the waiting room until they knew more.

When she stepped into his room, Mark was lying under a white sheet, his eyes closed, his breathing shallow. There were dark circles under his eyes. The nurse sat beside him, a white basin in her lap.

The sight of Mark lying there, pale and unmoving, jerked Kate out of the fuzzy confusion in her head. She leaned over and kissed his cheek.

"I'm here, Mark. Everything is going to be all right. You just have to rest and get well." She hoped that was true. It was *going* to be true. She stood up straight with sudden resolve. If she believed hard enough that Mark would get better, he would.

Back in the waiting room, she sat down on one of the hard, plastic chairs and leaned her head back. Sue was using the pay phone to call Jerry, and after a short conversation, she came back to say that the kids were fine. They'd been fed, and Lily had read them a story and gotten them to bed.

A sudden thought struck Kate, now that her brain was semi-functioning again. "But Sue, what about your kids? Who's with them?"

"My mother. Remember, she's here visiting? Don't worry, she raised six kids. Nothing fazes her." She got up. "I'm going to get some coffee and sandwiches. I'll be right back."

Kate didn't remember missing dinner, but now she realized that her stomach was very empty. She drank the coffee Sue brought back and nibbled on one of the sandwiches, then sat watching the clock on the wall, ticking off the minutes.

Hal suddenly appeared in the doorway. "Kate, Dick Halloran, the neurosurgeon, is here. He's seen Mark and looked at the x-rays, and he believes Mark has had an epidural hematoma. He's on his way to surgery right now."

Kate stood up and Hal took her arm to steady her. "What kind of surgery? What's the doctor going to do?"

"He has to remove the blood that's collecting under the membrane covering the brain. The sooner the better." He tightened his grip on Kate's arm. "Dick's an excellent surgeon and it's good that he's getting to Mark right away. It's crucial to a good recovery."

Kate's thoughts were whirling, and she grabbed one as it flew by. "Will Mark be all right? What's the prognosis?" Her knees were suddenly wobbly, and she sat down abruptly.

Hal nodded. "We certainly hope so. Say your prayers." He turned to Sue. "You can go on home, honey." He brushed his lips across her hair. "I'm having the nurses set Kate up in the room across from Mark, which luckily is empty at the moment."

Sue bent over and hugged Kate. "Don't worry about the kids. Lily will sleep at your place and call Jerry and Earl if either of them wakes up. I'll check on them in the morning." She turned at the door. "Try to get some sleep!"

"Sue's right, Kate. Mark will be in recovery for a while after the surgery, and they may not bring him back down here until morning. You might as well get some rest. Do you want something to help you sleep?"

Kate shook her head. "No, but thanks. I'll be okay."

"Well…all right then. Tell the nurse if you change your mind. It's my turn for the night shift so I'll be here all night. See you in the morning."

Kate did her best to take Sue's advice. The nurse had left a hospital gown and a thin cotton robe on the bed, but Kate just kicked off her shoes and crawled under the blanket. But instead of sleeping, she ended up lying awake, listening for sounds in the hall, getting up now and then to look over at Mark's door, as if she could see through it for signs that Mark was there.

Finally morning came. Hal was there first thing. Kate had already gotten up, splashed water on her face, smoothed her wrinkled skirt and blouse, and was sitting on a chair beside the door.

"Morning, Kate. Did you get some sleep?"

"A little." She rubbed her eyes. "How's Mark?" Her words stumbled over each other.

"Is he back yet? Is he okay?"

"Yup, he's here. The surgery went well, but he hasn't regained consciousness yet. Come on in with me and give him a morning kiss."

The smell of antiseptic and vomit rose to meet her in Mark's room. Mark was lying as she'd last seen him, pale and unmoving, with a white gauze bandage wrapped around his head. She kissed his forehead and murmured, "Good morning, my love." Mark didn't stir.

With his stethoscope Hal listened to Mark's heart and lungs. "Good. All okay." He straightened up.

"We'll be keeping a close eye on him today and hope he wakes up. Why don't you go home and get some rest?"

"No, I'll stay, if Sue and Jerry can manage the kids for a while longer."

"Okay, but I want you to at least go home for the night tonight. No arguments! You'll need to sleep. I'll call you if anything changes."

He turned back at the door. "I'm off today after rounds, but back tonight. I probably won't see you till tomorrow. Don't worry! Mark'll be all right. He's young and healthy and had very quick medical intervention. Lots of pluses!" He waved and disappeared.

Kate sat holding Mark's hand and talking to him softly, telling him about Sue and Jerry looking after things at home, and taking good care of Robin and Nora. One of the nurses brought coffee and asked if she'd like some breakfast, but Kate said no. She kept watching Mark's eyes, praying they'd open.

Sue called later in the morning and said she had picked up the children from Jerry and brought them to her house. "With my mother here with me and the five kids, what's two more?" she said.

Kate stayed at Mark's bedside all day, except to go to the cafeteria briefly for another cup of coffee and a salad. Sue appeared in the late afternoon.

"Hal says I'm to take you home. Doctor's orders. Earl drove me. He's out in the car waiting."

Kate stood up and reluctantly slipped her feet into her shoes. But she knew Sue was right. She suddenly felt overcome with exhaustion.

She leaned over and kissed Mark. "I'll be back soon, Mark. I'm just going home to check on Robin and Nora." She looked for some sign he heard, but his eyelids didn't flicker, and he slept on.

Earl stopped at Sue's so they could pick up the children. Robin was waiting on the front stoop, and when he saw Kate, he charged out and threw himself into her arms. She hugged his little body hard and then lifted Nora from Sue's arms, swallowing the tears that threatened to come.

"You can't imagine how glad I am to see you! I missed you so much," she said.

Robin reared back so he could see her face. "Where's Daddy?"

"He's still in the hospital and right now he's taking a nap. He needs to get lots of rest so he can get better."

Sue had explained to him that Mark had been in a bus accident and hurt his head, so now he asked, "Does his boo-boo hurt, Mommy?"

"I expect it does, but they have medicine at the hospital for that." She set him down and shifted Nora to her other hip. "Come, Earl's going to drive us home. Can you say thank you to Sue and Grandma Collins?"

Back at home, Kate found a pan of lasagna covered in foil on the kitchen table, with a note from Marge. "Here's your dinner, kiddo. Salad in the ice box. Call if you need anything." Again, Kate had to fight down tears. Sue, Jerry, Marge, Hal, Earl. Pitching in to help when she needed it most. With all their parents living hundreds or thousands of miles away, they were all each other's families.

Before she got into bed, she called the floor nurse. Mark was still not awake. There had been no change.

CHAPTER TWENTY-FOUR

Sue was there first thing the next morning and took the children home with her. As they left, Robin looked back at Kate. His little face was forlorn, and his eyes looked suspiciously wet. "'Bye, Mommy." He broke away from Sue and ran back to give Kate another hug.

"Hey, Robin," said Sue. "Guess what we're doing today. Grandma Collins is baking cupcakes and we're going to decorate them with frosting and sprinkles and eat them for lunch." She took Robin's hand. "So let's go see if they're ready yet."

Robin's face brightened and after one more backward glance he trotted off with Sue, clinging to Nora's stroller. Kate blew him a kiss. "Have fun! See you later."

While she waited for a cab, Kate knocked on Jerry's door to thank her for taking care of the kids. "I'm lucky to have friends like you, Jerry," she said. "I hope you didn't overdo. Those two can be a handful."

"We was fine, don't worry. How's Mark?"

"No change yet, but we're hoping. I'm on my way to the hospital. Sue's got the kids."

During the cab ride, Kate steeled herself for whatever awaited her. Good news or bad? She'd soon find out.

Mark was just as she'd left him the afternoon before. A still figure, eyes closed, brown hair tousled below the bandage.

She kissed his cheek, smoothing down his hair, then sat holding his hand. Hal came in a few minutes later. "Hi Kate. Did you get some sleep?"

"Actually, I did. I suddenly realized how tired I was. It's good you sent me home."

"Glad to hear it. Now let's see how this guy is doing this morning." He listened to Mark's heart and lungs, as he'd done the day before, and again he pronounced everything okay. He hung his stethoscope around his neck and started to straighten up, then stopped suddenly. "Hey, what's this? Mark, are you finally waking up?"

Mark stirred and tried to open his eyes. "Katie?" he mumbled.

Kate squeezed Mark's hand harder as Hal leaned closer. "She's right here, pal. You've had yourself a nice knock on the head, but how 'bout if you wake up now?"

Mark's lips moved as he tried to speak. "Aches." He put his hand up to his head. "Head aches."

"Yes, I know. It will for a while. I'll go order some pain medication for you right now. Behave yourself till I get back!" He patted Mark on the shoulder and gave Kate a big smile. "Good sign," he said "Very good sign. Be back in a minute."

Mark was trying again to talk. "So sorry, didn't mean…" His voice trailed off.

"It's all right. Whatever it is, stop worrying. Just take it easy and rest." She kissed him. "I love you, Mark."

"Love you…" His eyes closed and he seemed to be sleeping again.

Hal returned with the nurse and she gave Mark a shot for his pain. "He'll probably be in and out all day, maybe longer," Hal said. "But I think we're on the mend now. I'll be back to check on him later."

As Hal had predicted, Mark continued to fade in and out of consciousness all day and all night, and into the third day. But that afternoon, as Kate sat beside him reading a magazine, his eyes flew open. They were clear and focused. "What's going on? Kate? Where am I?" He tried to sit up.

"You're in the hospital," Kate said soothingly. She pushed him gently back down. "You have to lie down. You were in an accident and hurt your head. But you're getting better. Hal will be here soon, and you can ask him about it."

Mark frowned. "My head hurts."

"I know. Shall I call the nurse?"

Mark nodded. "I guess so." He was quiet a minute. "Where are the kids?"

"Sue and Jerry and Lily have been taking turns looking after them. They're fine. Robin misses you. He asks for you every day. He'll be so glad you're getting better."

Mark squeezed her hand. "I'm glad you're here, Katie," he said. "And I'm so sorry about this morning."

This morning? "Mark, what day do you think it is?"

He thought a moment. "Thursday?"

"No, it's Sunday. You've been in a coma for three days."

Mark shook his head. "Three days…What happened? Last thing I remember is being on the bus."

"The bus had an accident. It ran off the road and some of the students were injured, including you. They brought you here, and luckily Hal was on duty. He's been taking care of you."

Mark closed his eyes. "An accident…" His voice sounded sleepy and he drifted off again.

Kate spent most of the next two days at the hospital, as Mark gradually emerged from his mental fog. On the third day, when she opened the door to Mark's room, he was sitting in a chair by the window, reading the newspaper. A vase of red carnations on the windowsill sent waves of fragrance through the room. Kate wondered briefly if they were from Amanda.

Mark greeted her triumphantly. "My headache is gone! And I can actually think without feeling like my brain is full of fuzz. Hal says I can go home in a few days! How about a big hug to celebrate?"

"That's wonderful! I'm so glad you're better." He looked bright and alert, the old Mark before the accident. "Thank God. It's what I've been waiting for. Robin too. He can't wait to see you."

Kate reached down to hug him.

"Where'd the flowers come from? They're beautiful."

"The guys in the study group sent them. They came this morning." Mark patted the bed beside him. "Come sit, Katie," he said. "We need to talk. It's about Amanda. It's the first thing I thought of when I woke up. I've put it off way too long."

Kate's heart jumped. "Are you sure you're up to it?" Much as she'd tried to have this conversation, it didn't seem important anymore. Maybe they should wait until Mark was fully recovered.

"No, I'm okay. I want to talk. When I was riding the bus home the other day, before the accident, I decided it was time to explain to you about Amanda. So when I woke up this morning and I could actually function, the first thing I thought of was clearing the air about her."

He sighed. "It goes back to last semester when Amanda started out flirting with me. I tried not to encourage her, but I have to admit that I was flattered." He scowled in disgust." I let it go on too long. I was even stupid enough to let her talk me into meeting at her apartment, supposedly to study, but she met me at the door and before I knew what was happening, she was kissing me. I pulled away as fast as I could and left. But God, I felt so guilty."

He looked up at Kate, trying to assess her reaction. She frowned, and just shook her head.

Mark's words began to pour out faster and faster. "After that, I tried not to rock the boat in the study group by antagonizing her, but then she started asking me to help her with assignments and coach her before exams. I did help her a few times, but then I told her I couldn't do it anymore. I have a hard enough time getting my own work done. She kept asking, though. She doesn't give up."

"Maybe it was just an excuse to spend time with you." Kate shrugged. "I wouldn't put it past her."

"I don't know. Maybe" He looked at Kate apologetically. "I'm sorry. I've been such a jerk. I should have told you all this stuff sooner, but I was embarrassed, and I didn't know if you'd believe me. I was hoping the whole thing would go away and I wouldn't have to deal with it. Like I used to do with my mother. Big mistake."

"Yes, it was!" But she couldn't help it; there was relief in her voice. "I didn't know what to think and you seemed so evasive." She hesitated for a moment. "I thought you were falling for Amanda and weren't telling me. I even thought you might be having an affair. I tried not to believe it, but it was always there, haunting me, and it really, really hurt... So why tell me now?"

"Because something happened the day of the accident. I didn't even remember it at first, but it started coming back to me this morning when my head cleared." He drew a deep breath. "The thing is, Amanda is not as smart as she looks, or makes out. I don't know how she got into business school. Her father is an alum. Maybe he pulled some strings.

"Anyway, the day of the accident she offered to pay me to write her thesis—which is cheating, of course, but she doesn't care. She'll do anything to get what she wants. She followed me out of class and started arguing about it outside, in front of the graduate school. She was furious when I refused and walked away. I don't think she was ever denied anything in her life. It was all just handed to her."

So that's what the argument had been about.

"I actually saw you," Kate said. "I was in town on an errand, but I can't tell you about it yet. It's a secret." Mark looked at her questioningly, but Kate shook her head and interjected, "What do you mean about Amanda?"

"Well, for one thing, she told us one time in study group that she grew up in San Francisco, in Pacific Heights, which I guess is a pretty high-priced neighborhood.

"She's an only child, and her family must be wealthy, because every once in a while she drops little references about skiing at Lake Tahoe, or the Governor coming to dinner, or her friend at a private school in Switzer-land who was Princess Somebody-or-other.

Kate thought that this kind of background fit perfectly with what she knew of Amanda.

"But I guess it wasn't a very happy life in spite of all the money. Amanda mentioned one time that she'd spent all her summers at camp and the rest of the year in boarding school, and hardly ever saw her parents much. I guess she was pretty lonely.

"Anyway, when I said no to helping her write her thesis, she threatened

to tell you that we're having an affair. I told her you wouldn't believe her."
He stopped. "You wouldn't, would you?"

"Not if you said it wasn't true."

Mark looked relieved. "I don't know if she'll follow up on her threat, but if she does, it will be pure spite, just to get back at me."

Kate straightened up. "Don't worry, I can deal with Amanda." She looked him straight in the eye. "But if you had told me all this sooner, it would have saved me a lot of heartache. I wish you had trusted me to understand." Her look was somber.

"I know. I'm sorry." Mark looked at her pleadingly. "But I would never cheat on you, Kate. I love you."

Kate nodded slowly "Yes…I think you do."

Mark squeezed her hand. "I don't deserve you."

"Probably not," Kate said with the hint of a smile. "But it looks like I'm stuck with you."

She reached down and kissed him, then laid her cheek against his. She believed he was telling her the truth. Amanda had finally become a non-issue.

CHAPTER TWENTY-FIVE

MARK CAME HOME A FEW DAYS LATER, HEADACHE FREE BUT STILL A LITTLE weak. It seemed strange to have him there during the day. Robin loved it. Kate had to remind him that Daddy was still getting well and couldn't get down on the floor to build block towers or play race cars. She had called the plant the day after the accident and been told that Mark could come back to work as soon as he was able. They'd miss the three weeks of income, but she'd figure out something. She could save Laundromat money by washing not just the diapers but all the laundry in the deep side of the kitchen sink and hanging them outside on the line. And cut the food budget even further, with lots of mac and cheese and hot dogs. Ugh. She hated hotdogs, but at least they were cheap. If worse came to worst, she could ask her parents for another small loan.

By the second week Mark was getting restless, anxious to get back to work and school. He'd been studying for the final exam he'd missed and had also been helping Kate by propping his typewriter on a kitchen chair in the garden and working while Nora and Robin played. It provided Kate with the rare luxury of free time to do errands, get groceries, or do some work for the Town Committee.

The day he went back to school, Kate stood at the door and watched him striding down the street, swinging his new briefcase and limping a little from the old Army injury. She was thankful he'd recovered from the accident, but she'd miss having him around.

They'd had a delayed quiet birthday celebration for Mark, just the four of them, with Robin helping to stir the cake and wrap the briefcase in blue tissue paper. Both had been a big success.

That night, after the children were in bed, Mark pulled Kate down beside him on the couch. "I'm afraid Amanda's been stirring up more trouble."

What now? Kate thought.

"This morning between classes I took the bus to the other side of town, to a secondhand bookstore where I thought I could find a book I needed. As I was coming back, I saw Amanda through the bus window, coming out of a motel with our accounting professor."

"Dr. Schwartz.?" Kate's mouth hung open in surprise. "But he's married! I met his wife one time. She's really nice."

"I know. And Dr. Schwartz is a really good guy too. I can't imagine how Amanda managed to get her hooks into him, but apparently, she did. I don't think he saw me, but I'm pretty sure Amanda did."

"But what would she want with a middle-aged married college professor?" Kate was still trying to absorb the fact that Amanda was apparently not after Mark but had set her sights on other prey.

"I can guess. She's on the verge of flunking out of the accounting course, especially since I stopped coaching her. She probably thought she could persuade Dr. Schwartz to change her grades. I don't like to believe he would, but you never know. Men can be real jackasses sometimes." His smile was rueful. "So I'm guessing more recently her apparent interest in me was a smokescreen to hide her affair with Professor Schwartz. What an idiot I've been."

Kate pulled back a little and looked up at him. "Well...it does sound like something Amanda would do. But are you going to do anything about it? Talk to anyone?"

"I don't know. It wouldn't do any good to talk to Amanda. She doesn't listen to anybody. And I don't really want to tell Dr. Lehman. It would be the end of Dr. Schwartz's career." He sighed. "Maybe he'll come to his senses and break it off before someone else finds out."

Later, in bed, Kate's last thought was a wish that Amanda wouldn't ruin Dr. and Mrs. Schwartz's lives the way Kate had been afraid she'd ruin hers.

———

Kate started the class in constitutional law later in the week. She was excited about being back in school, challenging her brain to come awake again as she immersed herself in the intricacies of historic cases and Supreme Court decisions. The first day she walked into class, Dr. Washburn had greeted her warmly, but she felt nervous, nevertheless. She hadn't been in a classroom in more than three years, and even though she was only auditing, she wondered what she was doing here with all these young undergraduates. But when Dr. Washburn began the discussion of Marbury vs Madison, the crucial case that established the right of judicial review, she forgot her nervousness and listened intently to the discussion. After class, two of the other women introduced themselves and they walked out together, bemoaning the number of cases they had to study before the next class. Nervousness gone, Kate felt she was back in her element.

The date for the Town Democratic Committee picnic was set for a Saturday in mid-September. The day before the picnic, Kate made a big potato salad as requested by Barbara, who was organizing the food. Several people had volunteered to wheel their barbecues to the picnic, others were bringing little hibachi grills to make sure they could cook enough hot dogs. A sub-committee had set up two folding tables from the Community Center to hold all the food, and Kate had helped decorate them with red, white, and blue crepe paper and balloons. The weather was perfect, with blue skies, a warm sun and from somewhere a cool breeze.

Kate had gone next door and invited Earl and Jerry to go with her and Mark. "We're taking Robin and Nora too, so bring Lily and Danny along."

"Jesus, Kate!" Earl had looked at her in exasperation. "You trying to make a Democrat outta me? Jerry's been nagging me to register, and now she wants to go to this damn fool picnic."

"Oh come on, Earl. It's just a picnic. It won't hurt you to come. You might even enjoy it."

"Women!" he grunted.

Kate's mother had sent her a full-skirted red dress and red sandals to wear to the picnic.

"Nothing like a new dress to give you a lift," she'd written. "Now you can wow them all, including Senator Moody." Kate thanked the weather gods that it was warm enough to wear it.

Her parents had been enthusiastic supporters of her political activities and had even sent donations to the committee and to the senator's campaign. Kate felt a surge of gratitude as she slipped the new dress over her head. Her mother was right. She felt her spirits rise as she surveyed herself in the mirror. Not bad, she thought.

Mark let out a whistle. "Hey, glamour girl, time to go. You look gorgeous!"

Earl was bringing the coolers in his truck, so the rest of them walked over, across the field. The crowd on the Community Center lawn was in a festive mood. Someone had taped a poster of Senator Moody to the edge of the makeshift platform, and Jim had gotten the local high school band to come and play patriotic tunes and marches—loud and slightly out of tune, but they added to the holiday spirit. Kate and Mark and the Homans found a place to sit on the grass and eat, and as soon as Danny and Robin had finished their hot dogs—mustard smeared liberally on their faces—Lily had taken them to play on the swings.

Senator Moody had accepted the invitation to attend, and after most people had finished eating, he began to speak. He was a handsome, young-looking 50-year-old, a former college athlete who spoke eloquently about his platform. He was a strong supporter of civil rights, he declared, and vehemently opposed to Senator Joseph McCarthy's anti-communist crusade.

Kate could see Earl frowning and shaking his head when the senator spoke of equal protection for minorities. "I don't go along with that desegregation stuff," he said, when the senator finished to loud applause. "How you gonna enforce it? We got all them Jim Crow laws in Tennessee that's been around for years. People ain't going to want to change that."

"You have to start somewhere," Mark said. "It won't happen in a hurry, but if people like Senator Moody and Governor Stevenson get elected, at least we might make a start."

Earl shrugged. "Maybe. But I wouldn't count on it."

Jerry surprised Kate by speaking up. "It ain't right, treating coloreds the way they do in the South. We had a real nice colored family living near us back home and I always felt bad for the way folks looked down on them. You know that's true," she said to Earl. "Some people were right ugly to them and they didn't deserve it."

"Yeah, I know. But that way of lookin' at things ain't going away soon."

By now long shadows were creeping across the grass. Kate began collecting blankets, diaper bag, and children's toys. Jerry had gone to call Lily and the little boys. Almost all the other families had left when Kate noticed a stylish blond in a white sharkskin suit and high heels picking her way toward them.

"Amanda!" she exclaimed.

Mark had been folding one of the blankets. He stopped with it draped over his arm, a look of surprise on his face.

"What's up, Amanda? What are you doing here?"

"I was on my way to the airport when I saw your Democratic posters along the road. I knew you'd be here, so I thought I'd stop by to thank you for getting me expelled from school." Her green eyes were blazing. "I know it was you. You saw me that day coming out of the motel. And by the way, Dr. Schwartz is losing his job, also thanks to you."

"Sorry, it wasn't me." Mark's gaze was steady, his voice calm. "Someone else must have found out about you and Dr. Schwartz." He shook his head. "I'm sorry about Dr. Schwartz."

Amanda's voice rose. "Liar! You were jealous because I broke up with you." To Kate she almost shouted, "We were having an affair. All the times you thought he was studying in the library he was with me in my apartment. Your husband is not as perfect as you think."

"I know all about you and Mark, Amanda, and I don't believe a word you say." Kate's voice was firm. "So please just go away and leave us alone."

"Don't worry, I'm leaving. Daddy's sending me to Paris to work in his office there. He knows this whole thing is not my fault. They just don't want a woman in the MBA program."

She lifted her chin. "So I'm off to Paris. Au revoir—though I doubt whether we'll ever meet again."

And with that she turned to leave. One of her spike heels stuck in the grass and she stopped to yank it out, then limped back to the cab, shoe dangling from her hand.

Earl had been standing by, watching with interest. "Nice friends you two got," he observed. "Glad I don't have no college friends like that one."

Kate watched the cab disappear down the street. Paris. In spite of its European glamour and sophistication, Kate felt a little sorry for Amanda. She remembered what Mark had said about her lonely childhood—the poor little rich girl who probably didn't know what love is. Beneath her conniving behavior, maybe she was just seeking love. Maybe she'd find it in Paris.

Either way, as far as Kate was concerned, Paris was the best place for Amanda—far away on the other side of a big ocean.

POSTSCRIPT

Willow Run Village
June, 1953

ONCE AGAIN, KATE STOOD GAZING OUT THE KITCHEN WINDOW WHILE SHE lifted the last of the breakfast dishes out of the soapy water. Through the window she could see the ugly coal box in front, and the row of dreary buildings across the street. But today bright sunshine streamed through the window and turned to flame the red geraniums she had set in a planter on the stoop. She'd been inspired by the neighbor down the street who had done the same last summer. And if she turned her head, the view through the open living room door revealed not endless stretches of weedy fields, but green grass the color of spring, and Jerry's flamboyant petunias along the fence. A few weeks ago Earl had planted a little redbud tree at one corner of the garden, and it had valiantly put out a flurry of new apple-green leaves. By next spring, Earl had promised, it would be covered with delicate pink cotton-ball blossoms. Kate's spirits lifted at the sight of the garden, soul-nourishing and beautiful.

But she wouldn't be here to see it next spring. Mark had graduated at the end of May and had flown to San Francisco for an interview at the University of California Berkeley. At the suggestion of his advisor, Dr. Lehman, he'd applied for a job as an Administrative Officer in one of the university's big research centers.

With Dr. Lehman's excellent recommendation and Mark's impressive grade average, the interview went well. The result had been an offer of a job, starting right away. Mark had asked for time to consider and discuss it with Kate, but it hadn't taken them long to decide.

"The salary's enough for us to live on, and the prospects for advancement are there," Mark had said. "Besides, I like the idea of being in an academic atmosphere where I'll have a chance to help develop new programs and figure out how to finance them. And think of the climate compared to Michigan!"

"It sounds wonderful!" Kate stood quite still, trying to absorb it all. "Professor Washburn says the University of California Berkeley has an excellent political science department, and that with my grades, I shouldn't have any problem transferring."

They had looked at each other, eyes wide with excitement. "Then let's do it!" Mark grabbed her in a hug and danced her around the living room. Kate's insides churned with a mix of emotions: happy anticipation of a new place, a new life, yes. A degree of apprehension at the prospect of packing them all up and moving a couple of thousand miles away. Sadness at leaving her friends in Willow Run, and her garden, and at putting even more distance between her parents and her.

But as their plans had taken shape, her worries disappeared. She was accepted at Berkeley; Mark flew back to California and found them a tiny house in the Berkeley hills near the University. From the pictures Mark took, it looked like a magical tree house, a narrow two-story building with a garage at ground level and a wooden staircase to the balcony of the two-bedroom apartment perched among the trees. Mark's new employers would cover the cost of packing and moving them west. They would be able to afford child care for the children on the days when Kate had classes, and they could walk to the University while they saved up for a car. Robin was thrilled at the idea of flying. Every day he coaxed, "Can we go up in the airplane today, Mommy?"

Peg had typically shown up without warning, just in time to watch Mark process down the aisle in cap and gown to receive his degree. Mark had sent her an invitation, but after months of silence, he and Kate had not expected her to come. When Kate asked her how things were going, she said she and Doris had decided that Peg would stay on and be Doris's companion, helping with grocery shopping, driving to doctor appointments, maybe going on little outings on days when Doris was feeling up to it.

"Good riddance to Robert!" she told Kate. "Doris and I get along fine. We both like to play bridge, we like the same movies, like the same things to eat, what's not to like?"

She patted her tight blond curls. "Robert can go fly a kite as far as I'm concerned. He's a nitwit, if you ask me, traveling around in that little trailer like a gypsy and staying in crummy trailer camps. Not for me, thank you."

Robert had not come to the graduation. He was spending several months at a campground near San Diego and seemed happily content with the life he'd chosen. He had written that he'd drive north to visit once Kate and Mark were settled in Berkeley.

As she put the last dish away, Kate heard Danny talking to his mother out on the stoop, and Jerry answering in her unmistakable Tennessee drawl. Jerry was one of the people she'd miss—and Earl and Lily too. She marveled at the change in Jerry in the past year-and-a-half. She'd become an avid reader and regular visitor to the library with Lily. The last book she'd read had been *Gone With the Wind,* and when she finished it, she came next door to discuss it with Kate.

"I never knew 'bout all that stuff about the Civil War and what it was like afterward for the white people and former slaves. I never got enough school to learn much about history." Her green eyes were intent on Kate's. "What do you think about the way them—those—Yankees treated Southerners after the war?"

"I think some people in Washington meant for the ex-slaves and the white Southerners to be treated fairly. But then men from the North, called Carpetbaggers, took away some of the Negroes' rights and grabbed plantations away from Southern whites. It was shameful."

Jerry nodded. "Sure sounds like it. And what about Rhett Butler? Was he a good guy or a bad guy, do you think?"

"I think he was a little of both, but mostly good by the end of the story."

"Yeah…but I wish he and Scarlett had gotten together again at the end. Seemed like she changed too. But maybe too late." Jerry sighed. "Anyway, I'm glad I read it. I couldn't make out all the words, but Lily helped me. We stayed up way too late some nights, because we didn't want to stop reading." She smiled at Kate. "Never thought I'd end up reading a book like that. Or reading at all. We've got a new book out now, *The Adventures of Tom Sawyer.* Lily has to read it for school, so we're going to read it together."

Jerry had not only turned into a devoted reader, but she was actually being asked to be soloist at some of the churches in town. Word had gotten around among the various choir directors, and her first invitation had come in the spring. Jerry had hurried next door in a panic.

"I can't go sing in some church where I don't know nobody, and where a lot of them are probably professors or students from the University. What would they want with somebody from Tennessee who's never been to school to speak of?" She had the frightened rabbit look she'd had when Kate first knew her.

"Nonsense, Jerry. You have a glorious voice and you should share it with other people who will appreciate it. Of course you must do it. I'll go with you. Don't worry, you'll do fine."

With some extra urging from both Kate and Earl, Jerry gave in. The first time she sang at the Congregational church, something un-heard-of happened: people clapped at the end of her solo. Jerry stood in front of them, her face pale, tears in her eyes.

"They liked my singing!" she said later to Kate and Earl. "No one ever clapped for me before." She shook her head in disbelief.

She was still frail, and had to rest for a while every afternoon, but her skin had a healthier pink glow these days, she stood up a little straighter, and most of the time she had lost that frightened look

She had been guest soloist several times since, both at the Congrega-tional Church and at others. "Did you know they pay me to come?" she asked Kate. "Pay me money to *sing*! They wouldn't need to. I'd sing just for the pure pleasure of it."

And it's made you happy, Kate thought. What a blessing that Marge suggested she go to church with me that first Sunday.

She'd miss Barbara too. They had become good friends and met frequently for lunch after class when Mark and Barbara's husband were too busy to join them. They talked about their classes, about politics, about the recent presidential election when Stevenson had lost to Eisenhower.

"We lost a good man," Barbara mourned. "But maybe he'll run again, and we'll get another chance to campaign for him."

When Kate told her they were moving to California, she said, "So see that you get involved in the la la land of California politics, and join the Democratic Town Committee out there. If there isn't one in Berkeley, I'm counting on you to start one!"

Annie and John had moved to New York City after John graduated in January. The goodbyes had been stiff. Kate had called Annie to wish her luck in their move, and Annie had answered coolly. "I won't miss anything about this miserable place," she said. "The sooner we're out of here, the better. Goodbye, Kate."

Kate hung up the dish towel and joined Mark and the children in the garden. Nora was toddling around on shaky legs, chewing on a fistful of grass and plopping down like a fat rubber ball whenever she lost her balance. Mark was in the sandbox with Robin, making car tracks in the sand.

"Sue called. She says the date for our farewell party is this Saturday night. She's organizing all the food. I said I'd make strawberry shortcake for dessert."

Sue and Hal, Kate thought with a pang. The two of them had been her rock whenever she needed them. She'd miss them most of all. Sue had promised they'd visit--she and Hal had always wanted to see California, and anyway, who knows, they might end up there permanently. Hal would finish his residency in August and was already applying for jobs. He'd put in an application at the UCSF, the University of California at San Francisco Medical School, and was waiting to hear back. What unbelievable luck if it turned out that he and Sue would be in San Francisco--right across the bay from them.

The night of the party, Kate put on her red dress and matching sandals and fastened her grandmother's pearls around her neck. GeeGee had given them to her on her eighteenth birthday. Stepping over to the mirror, she admired their soft shine against her red dress.

She was barely ready when guests began to arrive. Sue bustled around the garden, setting up some folding tables and chairs that Hal had borrowed from the hospital, arranging the platters of food on the picnic table. Marge and Jake were among the first to arrive.

"Here's my usual lasagna," Marge announced. "It's among the few things I know how to cook. All Jake ever wants is meat loaf or pot roast, so it kinda limits my culinary repertoire." Jake shook his head at this regrettable lack of understanding of the male appetite and reached for a handful of potato chips.

It was quite a feast. That afternoon Kate had enlisted the help of Lily and Robin in hulling and washing several quarts of Michigan's finest strawberries, and had made two batches of biscuit shortcakes, baking them in shifts in the toaster oven. Jerry brought chili and Ruby some of her corn bread, Sue had contributed potato salad and Beth a large bowl of salad greens with her special dressing. Kate had invited Barbara too, and she hurried in a little late, carrying two bottles of wine.

The yard was full of children: Sue and Hal's five, Beth's little girl, Danny and Robin and Nora bobbing in and out between the adults' legs. After they'd been appeased with hot dogs from the grill, Lily gathered them all up and took them to the communal swing set in the middle of the field.

The adults sat around sipping wine, or the beer Earl had brought, and helping themselves to the spread on the picnic table. At one point, Hal raised his glass and said,

"Since we're here to say goodbye to Mark and Kate, let's wish them good luck as they shake off the coal dust of Willow Run Village and head to California!"

There was a murmur of congratulations, and then Ruby stood up. "I got somethin' I want to say to Kate, and I'm speakin' for Jerry too. Thanks to her, things has changed here on Raleigh Court since she come to my door that day." Kate put up her hand to stop her. "No Ruby..." but Ruby cut her off.

"It's the truth. I got friends now--you and Mark, and Jerry and Earl, and Marge and Sue and the doc. Me and Bert get together to play cards with Jerry and Earl real often, and Jerry comes over to my place and we bake and drink sweet tea and have a good gossip. And sometimes on Saturdays Marge gives me and Jerry a ride to the grocery store and we go someplace afterward for a sandwich or something. We never did none of that before, and you're the one started it. Jerry's too shy to say so in front of everybody, but she's thankful you got her to reading books and singing in choirs. We just wanted to tell you that." She sat down abruptly as though she had suddenly run out of breath.

Embarrassed and touched, Kate groped for words. Hal saved her by raising his glass and saying, "To Kate, who saw to it that we all became friends, and to Mark, who had the good sense to marry her and bring her to Willow Run!"

Sue got up to give Kate a hug, and then they were all hugging and laughing at once, together in Kate's garden for what they all knew would be the last time.

Kate looked around at the garden, at friends and flowers, at the little redbud tree that she would never see bloom and said a silent goodbye.

California was waiting.

ABOUT THE AUTHOR

Dorothy Stephens lives with her neurotic cat Chitty in Massachusetts, where she likes to walk along the ocean looking for inspiration for her next book. Her previous works include a memoir, Kwa Heri Means Goodbye; Memories of Kenya 1957-1959, and a YA novel, A Door Just Opened. Her articles, essays, and travel pieces have appeared in a number of national magazines and newspapers.

www.dorothystephens.com

facebook.com/dorothy.stephens.507

ALSO BY DOROTHY STEPHENS

With Fire & Ice Young Adult Books, an imprint of Melange Books, LLC

A Door Just Opened